Love Promises

Love Promises

A Novel

The Love Trilogy
3 of 3

Sherry Lucille

Inspiring Destiny Press
MADISON, WISCONSIN

Published by:
Inspiring Destiny Press, Inc.

www.sherrylucille.com

Cover art by Hannah Sandvold
hsgraphics.blogspot.com
hcsandvold@gmail.com

ISBN- 0692558209
ISBN- 9780692558201

LCCN:
Library of Congress Cataloging-In Publication Data
Lucille, Sherry
Love Promises: a novel/ by Sherry Lucille

ISBN-   ISBN-

1. Love-Fiction 2. Chicago (ILL.)--20th century--Fiction.
3. Nineteen sixties-Fiction. 4. Nineteen seventies-Fiction. I. Title.

Printed in the Unites States. First Edition

Thanks to Him who sees me, El Roi!

Special thanks to:

A Place At The Table - my creative sisters who help me to take flight

Thanks to my friend Sharyl Kato, who is third generation Japanese American. She read a draft of my novel and gave it a thumbs up!

Thanks to my young friend Stella who sat with me one day and shared with me her perspective on being biracial: Japanese/White in America. This helped me to have a greater understanding of a biracial perspective less familiar to me.

Thank you, Keiva, for giving me honest and helpful critique. Thank you for being you.

To author Catrina J. Sparkman and teacher Stephanie Barnard for reading *Love Promises* in the early stages and telling me to "go head".

As always to My husband for Always being there
    My daughter for Strength
      My son for Joy

And to my entire natural and spiritual family for your steadfast support.

Diary of a Mad Kid 1949

I called her so loud my tonsils hurt. She was staring at me with her scary eyes. Just staring. Yucky red was everywhere. My heart was thundering, trying to get out of my chest. The door slammed. I jumped and turned around. Where can I hide? My hands had blood all over them. Maybe I can get to the closet. No, his feet are coming. Maybe under the bed? He's at the door. My stomach hurts so bad. I'm sorry. He ran at me and pushed me down. I didn't mean to... He didn't hear me. He didn't care. Get out! he yelled, I never want to... I wanted to scream. My face is stinging, but I can't cry.

I think, I'm sick, and I'm never gonna get well.

Rustling in the Wind
1969

Cameron had seen it many times before. Dobbs would have Lois, his secretary, come in and tidy his office, removing all extraneous items so that every piece of research, every book, and every article pertaining to the client's business was prominently displayed. A note pad with a perfectly sharpened pencil next to it would be off to the right for jotting his secret shorthand. All of this was neatly arranged on his enormous wooden desk, which he used as a shield between himself and that client. Mason Dobbs, de facto Top Ad Man at Brandon & Dobbs, would be sitting behind that desk.

And today he'd be wearing his signature black suit jacket with sleeves too long for his short, stout arms and a wide necktie. Dobbs wasn't keeping up with the trends though. If he had perused the fashion section of *Life*, he would have known that

1969 was indeed the year of the wide tie. But unlike himself, Dobb's didn't see the benefit of knowing something about everything. His brush with fashion today was due to his secretary's machinations. Lois had purchased a tie for Mason Dobbs, their boss, to curry his favor, and one for him for an entirely different reason.

As Cameron neared Lois' door, he laughed, thinking people had a tendency to take the portly man lightly. Just because Dobbs was badly dressed and out of step didn't mean he was stupid. If Cameron were a betting man, he'd lay odds that in addition to his ordinary suit and blistering blue tie, their boss was wearing an impeccably well-constructed, crisp white shirt produced by the Colless family. And, he would be ready for this meeting with his brilliance firmly in place.

As soon as Cameron saw Robert Colless enter Dobbs' office, he quietly stepped into Lois' adjourning room, giving her "the signal." She winked and carefully pushed the intercom button.

"Mr. Dobbs, glad to meet you. Been looking forward to doing business with your firm for years. Finally got big enough to be able to afford Brandon & Dobbs, the best ad agency in the Midwest."

"You pay us a great compliment, Mr. Colless. We pride ourselves in being able to represent our clients in a way that makes them shine. We have a proven track record of increasing sales exponentially." Dobbs' voice was clear and vigorous. Cameron thought it exuded confidence. "We believe we can grow your sales by no less than 60% in the first year of being represented by Brandon & Dobbs. If we decide to work together, you will love the job we do for you."

"If? You do mean when?" Colless, baritone voice shaking, was not certain at all. Simply by listening through the intercom, Cameron imagined Colless' feet shuffling in black dress shoes he'd probably purchased specifically for this meeting.

"Mr. Colless, I must be frank with you. Our research department is still in the process of looking at your product. During our inquiries some disturbing things have been alleged about your private life. Any of which if proven true and brought to light, would make it hard, if not impossible, for us to do a good job for you. At Brandon & Dobbs, we take as much care selecting our clients as they do selecting us."

"Bull crap, there's not a company in the world that can't be bought. And besides, whatever you've heard is lies. That other stuff is family, not business."

"We will see. Anyway, let us get to the business at hand. I have two Ad Execs who are currently available and exceptionally capable of doing a wonderful job for you."

"I sure do hope one of them is that pretty little red head you got working here. Word is she's one of your top Ad men. You people are breaking some new ground here with a woman doing this kind of work."

"Yes, Miss Cole is an exceptional talent. We are fortunate to have an Ad Executive with her skills. Unfortunately she is not available. She is handling two national campaigns at the moment, but if you care to wait…"

"No, this can't wait. Gotta strike while the iron is hot. Who are these two dudes you think can handle my company?"

"Cameron O'Neil who's been with us for a few years and a more recent hire, Mark Schultz. Mark has impeccable judgment and Cameron has an extensive knowledge base, tending in all directions."

"Great, when can I meet them?" Colless spouted.

In the adjourning office, Cameron kissed Lois' hand. Then he slyly tested the space behind her corner file cabinet, just in case Robert Colless came out before he was done. Lois was always moving things around, trying to improve her systems as she called them.

"Mr. O'Neil, you are going to get me fired," she whispered releasing the button on the intercom, which allowed her to hear what was being said next door in her boss's office.

"Shhh," Cameron whispered sauntering over to where she was sitting and touching his finger to her mouth. She really was a good-looking woman, her blond hair matching the color of his. "I like it better when you call me Cameron. It sounds so pretty coming off your lips."

"Cameron." She pushed at his hand, causing file stacks to tumble from her desk and over his shoes. "If Mr. Dobbs knew I had his intercom on while he was in a private meeting, I'd lose my job, no matter how long I've worked for him."

"And who's going to tell him?" He gathered the folders from the floor and pushed at the knot on the wide tie she had given him. "It'll be our little secret," he sighed ogling her long legs spun out from under her desk in protest.

"Cameron," she surrendered, allowing her head to rest on her palm as she peered up at him from her rolling desk chair. "When did you say you were going to take me out to dinner?"

"I'll call you," he said. "Now remember," he moved very close to her lips again, "I was never here."

"Never here," she mouthed.

He had mesmerized tougher women than Lois with his "baby-greens" as his mother had called his sparkling eyes. Too bad the desire to have her or any of the Brandon & Dobbs women was beginning to lose its luster.

In the quiet of her office, Lois could hear the air moving from her employer's intercom to hers. Either party could open the channel by pressing the button.

"Miss Niffe."

"Yes, Mr. Dobbs?" Lois answered moving close to the box on her desk.

"Please let Schultz and O'Neil know that we will be meeting with Robert Colless next week, Monday at 3:00."

"Yes, sir. Will there be anything else?"

"Yes, I noticed the hiss of the open intercom during my last meeting..."

Lois held her breath. What now?

"Lois. . ," Mason Dobbs continued.

"Yes, sir?" her hand was shaking as she pressed her fist to her lips.

"If it happens again…"

"It won't, sir, I promise." She leaned back in her seat unable to move until her heart started beating again. Cameron might be the most gorgeous man she'd ever known, but something had changed. He was even less interested in her these days than he had been just months ago. He certainly was not worth going to the poor house over. There would be no more spying on Mr. Dobbs and no more special favors for Mr. O'Neil.

2:15 p.m. Cameron wound his watch to match the clock on his wall. Time for the meeting. It would have been just another dreary October afternoon for most of the office, Cameron thought, walking across the brightly lit maze of secretaries, copy editors, and artists, except everyone was still buzzing about the national guard being called out to quell demonstrations in the Loop last week. Students and other young people were protesting the trial of the "Chicago Eight" and the Vietnam War. That was followed by several more days of unrest downtown.

Colless was rumored to have made some disparaging remarks about Bobby Seale, over the weekend, at what he thought was a private party. Cameron's contact told him that the remarks were definitely not related to Seale's politics. Dobbs had to have also heard, and he was sure to ask Colless about it at their meeting today.

Nineteen sixty-nine was a year of struggle. How unfortunate for Colless that the struggle may have risen up to bite him in the butt. All because he didn't know when to keep his mouth shut. Cameron's thoughts, which he kept to himself, were that young men shouldn't fight old men's profit wars, hence his secure stay stateside.

Poor Colless, could he really be this foolish? Politics and social issues in general only mattered to Cameron as far as they affected the advertising landscape and his ability to do business in it. He had enough internal angst and upheaval to deal with. He'd let others work on the United State's national conscience regarding war, race, and the like. His contribution would be diversion. He'd use his personal charm and professional prowess to give people something else to think about. He laughed at his own hubris as he took the last steps toward Lois' desk; this was laying it on thick. And a schemer should never delude himself.

"Lois," he said sweetly when he was standing over her, just outside their boss's office. She refused to look at him. He shrugged, opened Dobbs' door, announced himself and walked in. Schultz was on his heels. (Poor Mark Schultz had been promised the promotion to partner months ago and it was still "in the making". Apparently Eric Brandon was loath to give up control after all.) He and Mark sat in the plush seats in front of Dobbs' oversized desk. These chairs were the most extravagant things in his office. Dobbs used them to disarm their clients, both on the professional and personal level. Cameron sat with Mason Dobbs and his rival, Mark Schultz, pouring over the Colless family product line of originally home-sewn business attire.

Cameron, always a man of impeccable dress, thought the workmanship was impressive and the product promising. With minor adjustments to design and the right ads, this product line appeal could be extended to some unexpected markets.

They were waiting for Robert Colless to arrive and give an account for himself. This was one of the things Cameron liked least about B & D, their high-mindedness. Why couldn't they just stick to advertising like everybody else in the field? If these new allegations proved true, Brandon & Dobbs would not be representing the man.

2:55 p.m. All three stood behind the desk. Dobbs flanked on either side by himself and Schultz. 3:00

p.m. Lois, cheeks tight and looking daggers at him, appeared to announce Robert Colless' entrance.

Colless shook their hands vigorously then stepped back admiringly. "Dobbs, these studs are on the wrong end of the business. Can I get one of them to model the clothes? We could get sales up 70% in the first year. I'm sure of it."

Schultz looked down, a brown curl obscuring his eyes: too humble. Cameron met the man's gaze. He smirked. He had been here before; being overtly admired for his looks was not new to him. "I'd be happy to represent your company, Mr. Colless, in whatever way makes sense. But we are in the ad business, modeling will have to wait."

"Uhh humm," Dobbs chimed in. "Let's not get ahead of ourselves. Tell us about your family's business, what do you have in mind as a way to get the attention you desire and who do you see us marketing this product to?"

"You want me to do all the work." Colless looked down shuffling his feet. "Well, let me see. Our company was started by us, an All-American family. Mother and father, three sons. Hard working every single one of us. We want our clothes to be worn by people like us."

Even Cameron couldn't help giving a knowing look at his co-workers. Everything Colless was saying was wrong. Robert Colless was known to have no employment other than being the eldest of the three sons. As soon as his mother died, he used his share of the "worthless" company's earnings to buy out his brothers' portion of their parents' business, which he probably told them was going nowhere; and here he was trying as hard as hell to make it go somewhere fast. Cameron could relate to this maneuver, but unless he had missed his guess, Colless was taking himself down the rabbit hole and only he was unaware of it.

"All-American, you say," Mark Schultz repeated. "Tell us more about that."

"Yes, of the three of us, Schultz would be most interested in that," Cameron erupted—uncharacteristically. Mark was married to a colored woman, one he himself had courted but would never have been foolish enough to marry. Cameron wondered how Dobbs was interpreting his outburst.

"Well, you know, your everyday American. Like you and me." Colless pointed between himself and them, collectively.

"Ahem," Dobbs interjected again, "how do you see us representing your clothing? It's business man's attire, correct?"

"Right you are." Colless shifted nervously. "My father used to say my mother sewed the collars of her shirts tighter than a noose. We had to tell her to loosen up. They're not for hangin' nig— Hey what are we talkin' here? That's why I came to you. You have a great reputation and— "

"And, we'd like to keep it that way," Schultz shot, glaring at Colless.

"Yes, we would," Dobbs said laying his hand on Shultz's sleeve.

"Mr. Colless, you've misjudged us," Cameron finished. Both Dobbs and Schultz eyed him suspiciously, like it wasn't in his nature to suggest passing on a lucrative account, no matter how odious the client.

Colless looked stunned at first. Then annoyed. "So you're turning me away? You don't want my business? Perhaps you don't know how much I'm prepared to pay you?"

"It's not a matter of money," Dobbs snapped.

"It's not, huh?" Colless looked around in disbelief. "Damned Communists. Why don't you fellas head on down to that courthouse where that Chicago Eight Trial has been going on. Get on down there and support that America-hating-brood. No wonder my mother had the good sense to die. It's all right. Smith and Olson will take me on. Hell, they 'bout begged me to come to them. I'll get the last laugh. Coulda' fooled me though. You guys sure don't look 'pink.' Wait till this gets out! Damn Commies, who knew!" He blew a huge sigh, ran his hand through his hair, turned and left.

For several minutes no one spoke. They all stood staring after Colless, arms folded, momentarily stunned themselves. Then they moved and turned to look at each other. "His briefcase," Mark sneered. "Apparently he was as shocked as we were. Someone should take it to him." He didn't move.

"I will," Cameron said. "We're still civilized aren't we? Just because the man's a racist doesn't mean we can't extend professional courtesy. Besides, we wouldn't want him to have to come back for it." No one disagreed. He picked up the case and ran.

Cameron raced down the muggy staircase that led to the side entrance and out into the bright but very chilly afternoon. He knew Colless would have likely taken advantage of their V.I.P. parking. He hiked up his collar and pulled his suit coat tight over his chest. He'd be cold but not for long. He made it just in time. Colless was turning the key in the door of his brand new silver Cadillac. The man hadn't wasted any time spending mommy's money.

"Mr. Colless!" Cameron called from a few cars down. He held the case high, waving it partly to get his attention and partly to stay warm.

"Well," Colless laughed, blowing into his hands, "at least you pinkos got common courtesy. Can't say it means a lot right now. Gimme that." He snatched his case from Cameron's hand and turned back to his car.

"Mr. Colless, wait," Cameron planted his hand on Colless' back.

"What you want, a date?" He looked over his shoulder. "I don't swing that way."

Cameron doubted that but stuck to the issue at hand. "I'm sorry about what happened up there."

"What? What are you saying?" Colless stood up straight, pushing his hands into his pockets and eyeing Cameron from head to toe.

"I said I'm sorry about what happened up there." Cameron was rubbing his hands together and shuffling from side to side to stay warm. "If you are still interested in having a member of Brandon & Dobbs represent you, perhaps we," Cameron moved in using a mock whisper, "you and I, could come to some agreement."

"Well, boy." Colless' smile lit his face as he grabbed Cameron by both shoulders peering at him. "I thought I saw something in you. What have you got in mind? Tell me, what are you thinking?"

Cameron was no fool. Green was the only color he had an allegiance to, and he hadn't survived all these years on good looks alone.

CHAPTER 1

Hello, Old "Friend."

"**P**erfidious peacock!" Emily Le'tille bellowed, her face beet-red and fist shaking, as Cameron fled the library like a thief in the night. He wasn't stealing. Those days were long behind him. No, he had injured her pride. The funny thing is, he hadn't even seen it coming. The incident had started innocently enough.

"This way, Mr. Cameron." He checked over both shoulders, though he knew she was talking to him. How did she know his name or what he wanted? "Your books on diamond-mining have been moved," Librarian Le'tille informed him. "Follow me." He started out walking slowly, a bit concerned as she shoved past bent-over Bagley, an unfortunate name given to a poor hunchback. It didn't occur to him until the third time she stopped short, in the narrow aisle; and he stumbled into her backside that his books had been intentionally moved to this dimly lit, obscure spot. "Mr. Cameron, please bring over that rolling ladder." Her rough fingers grazed his cheek when she reached up to get *The Diamond Mines of South Africa* by Gardner Williams, and she nearly kissed him when she turned to pick out *Earnest Oppenheimer and the Economic Development of South Africa*. But the kicker came when she hiked up her already-tight dishwater colored skirt and her dimpled thigh rubbed his shoulder as she climbed to retrieve Newberry's, *The Diamond Ring*.

"Cameron," she belched, "you wouldn't be getting married on me?" Miss Le'tille was an unkempt woman of an advanced age. Her roots were an inch of gray with a bad dye job and her lips sported a blotchy shade of pink. She was rude and too loud for her profession, and they had never been formally introduced, so he refused to be responsible for what was about to come out of his mouth.

"No, Miss Le'tille, I wouldn't be getting married 'on you,' under you, around you and certainly not to you." The first book flew fast, grazing his ear. The second like a rocket, came within an inch of his arm. There was a horrible thunder as she jumped from the ladder hurling another. He wobbled into a sitting patron as *The Diamond Ring* clapped his temple. Lecherous Le'tille was not done yet. To add insult to injury, as he fled, she yelped, "Find another library, you perfidious peacock!"

It wasn't the first time he'd been called a peacock. On January 3, 1955, his 16th birthday, Mildred Abusier, his benefactor, had pronounced him so. He was standing on the pedestal in the fitting room of Miche Clothier trying on his first tailor-fitted suit. It was a trim cut, dark gray. He thought it looked perfect with his spit-shined black shoes. "Our little man. All grown up," she gushed to Mrs. Burns. "And he wears it with relish and flair, does he not?" she punctuated as he turned from front to back admiring his reflection. His blond hair was freshly cut, longer on top and tapered at the neck and ears.

"Our perfect peacock," Mildred snickered, not caring if he heard. He didn't care. He liked what he saw. He fingered his tie absentmindedly as they paid the cashier and left.

Peacock, yes. But perfidious? He was not at all sure. Despite being a self-proclaimed wordsmith, he had never even heard the word. Let me see, Cameron pushed down into his sturdy and stiff couch, elbowing the pillows. Perfidious, perfidious . . . he licked his finger and began to page through his heavy dictionary and his even heavier thesaurus. Ah, here you are . . . deliberately faithless, treacherous, deceitful. *Ouch*. He yanked the knot of his tie roughly. Not only did Le'tille know his name, she knew his character.

On a roll, he flipped his notebook to a clean page and wrote out a few more definitions. Multifarious: having many different parts, elements, forms. Recalcitrant: not responsive to treatment. Humm, what was this beat-up-on-Cameron Day?

'God I hate you'

"Not today. I don't want to do this today!" Cameron hissed, jumping to his feet and pounding his temple with his fist. If he could crush **IT** out he would. Now he knew, it was beat-up-on-Cameron Day.

While pacing and trying to refocus, **IT** subsided. He sat, hard, trying to go back to his writing. No good. He flung his paper and pen onto his TV snack table and sunk into a pillow, casting a weary eye on his subdued apartment. One wall was completely covered by an old-but-able bookshelf—packed to bulging with books on zoology, carpentry, and etiquette. His square dinette with rounded corners and two metal chairs with vinyl-padded seats held books on travel to Malaysia, India, and Egypt. Still no books on the diamond industry. If only Le'tille had minded her own business, he'd be halfway through his research on the Levy account.

Feeling calmer, he sat back down again scanning his apartment. A small sink, slender counter, yellow stove with four burners and a fridge that worked perfectly, when the freezer wasn't caked with ice, occupied a back corner. No frills. He didn't want things.

His mind wondered back to Le'tille. She actually thought he might be getting married. No, that wasn't for him; but Mark's wife, Shelly, she was the type of woman a man wanted to marry. He knew that from the small amount of time he spent with her just over a year ago. She'd looked at him like he was more, more than the conniving, scheming man everyone knew him to be. And he, he had started to believe that could be true. A smile creased his lips. Could he have actually changed for her?

CHAPTER 2

Awakening

Diary: November 1, 1969

I think I'm ready to admit it. Life to date is crap. Nothing, and I do mean nothing, is working out the way I planned. It all just seems like some new kind of hell. Yesterday, what started with Le'tille's waft had immediately unleashed the torrent. This on top of everything...

Vying for this partnership at Brandon and Dobbs is like being in a prizefight: *And in this corner we have the amazing Amanda Cole, the woman who would be king! She has worked and schemed for years to win this, the coveted partnership. Not just for her but for all womankind. Ladies and gentlemen, that's what she'd like you to think, but Amanda Cole is the only woman Amanda Cole wants to get ahead. And in this corner is everyone's favorite, except for Mason Dobbs' of course. Cameron O'Neil is charming, brilliant, an artful fighter. He has schemed and worked for years to win this fight! The crowd goes wild. Wait a minute. Who's that? A third contender? Yes, I see a third, Johnny-come-lately Mark Schultz. He can't beat out Amanda and Cameron, can he? Look at all of the time and cunning they've put in.*

Ah yes, this is the rub, Mark Schultz is going to get it. The third contender who nobody saw coming is going to walk away with the prize.

They really got me this time. All of 'em', God, the devil, the Fates, anybody and everybody. They all stuck it to ol' Cam. Yes they did.

"Cameron O'Neil, what brings you out on such a fine day?" *See what I mean,* Cameron thought back to the journal entry he had written a week ago. No sooner had he reached the block leading to his office building, his nemesis howled. Cameron could hear the insincere greeting, but he could not yet see the man. He yanked his leather gloves onto his freezing hands and squinted.

Mark Schultz was dodging left and right in a small clearing between the Todd and Emerson office buildings. Crystal globs of snow fell from the clouds obscuring his face, soaking wet brown curls dripped from his forehead. Schulz looked like the abominable snow something or other, heading toward him shouting.

Just as Cameron was about to shout back, "What could that possibly matter to you?" he spied her elegant fingers curving around Schultz's waist.

"Hello, Cameron." Shelly's head popped from behind the massive heathen. Cameron shook his head, hard to believe, some women preferred savage beasts. That thought occurred to him as he watched her dance into view, her thin coat clinging to her still rounded body. How could he? How could Schultz let this goddess run around in this cold and slushy weather just months after giving birth? Cameron thought, *if she had married me she would have been inside, warm and safe.* Could she have really been his? Sweetly, she waltzed toward him with her hands stretched out. For what? A handshake? A friendly hug? Schultz's eyes narrowed. Even through the quickening flurry, Cameron could see his protective gaze.

Don't worry, I won't steal your little bride. Not today anyway. With a curt nod, he sidestepped the frolicking lovers, who, after sparing him a pitying glance, went back to their snow-play.

The thing Cameron had dreaded for months had come to pass. Mark Schultz had become a partner at his ad agency and thus his boss. The job apparently had its perks. Look at him laughing and whooping like a giant loon. We're in the ad business, for Pete's sake. What would people think if they saw Schultz out here making a spectacle of himself in the middle of the day? I ought to give him a piece of my . . . That thought died as quickly as it sprang. Cameron realized he no longer cared.

The closer Cameron got to the office the more stuck he felt. Soggy heaps of snow bombarded him, soaking him to his core. His feet became weights and his legs insubordinate children. Forward, he reproached them. Reluctantly, they obeyed right up until the moment he noticed that audacious sign. It was erected over the old one, which had stood for what? Close to two decades. Cameron shuffled his feet from side to side while pulling his lapel flaps together.

The bright red and blue moniker with its enormous gold lettering showed right through the drifting and blowing camouflage, taunting him: Dobbs, Schultz & Brandon. *"Ha, ha, what cha gonna do?"*

Blinding sun split the clouds. The snow stopped and began to disappear as quickly as it came. With his arms across his chest, he stood looking at the DSB sign until eyestrain set in. This was where he'd cut his teeth. This was the place from which he'd launch his empire. But in an instant, a flash, it was ripped from him. Mark Schultz, the real thief, had turned his world upside down.

Shivering, Cameron stripped his gloves from his hands and pulled a pack of cigarettes from his inside coat pocket, hit the packet on his stinging red knuckle and plucked one. He fumbled through his pocket, located his ice-cold silver lighter and flipped it open. He lit the tip of his cigarette and took several puffs before flicking half the tobacco roll into the air and hawking a blob of spit onto the ground. Ceremoniously ungentleman-like, but quite apropos given the circumstance.

Suddenly the dampness of his clothing was overwhelming. He removed his overcoat and ran for the side door. Taking the musty stairwell instead of the musty elevator was just the thing to get his ire up.

"Marge, get Dobbs out here immediately!" Cameron demanded bursting into the rear entry and landing just past "partition valley" where most of the secretaries, copy editors, artists and everyone not important enough to have an office resided.

He had been threatening to quit for months, but Marge, his faithful secretary, who was positioned right outside his office, was having none of it. Marge, who had been with him two years, was not his usual fare, even in secretaries. She was about fifteen years his senior, not too pretty but not hard on the eyes either. She was very efficient and caring. Too caring at times. She cared about the world, about B & D, and about him. It was the caring about him that both pleased and confused him. It was for this reason, he supposed, that he picked her up when Amanda Cole, B & D's only female executive, dismissed her.

"It's not a good time, Cameron," Marge shushed, draping his coat over her arm and completely ignoring his request for a meeting with Dobbs. "Mr. Dobbs says you're late for the Imperial Shipping meeting." She sniffed him and asked why he had picked up that despicable habit again. He should have fired her on the spot.

He wanted to turn something over, cause some kind of upheaval. Maybe he'd spit right there on that dime-store carpet, but that would have been taking the Humphrey Bogart act too far. He chuckled, thinking of the ladies passing out en masse as he let a wad fly: a perfect display of disrespect and vulgarity. Everything he was feeling these days. Restraining himself, he marched into his office giving Marge a grimace as he passed.

Dobbs would have to wait. He plopped into his doughy maroon wheeled-chair searching his desk for his diary. Finding it, he breathed deeply, propped his feet on his desk and glanced sideways out his only window. It sported a wonderful view of a brick wall. He was glad he had refrained from doing anything rash like quitting or vulgar like spitting. The disrespect would not shock the ladies, but vulgarity coming from the proper Mr. O'Neil certainly would have. He wasn't done here yet. He might get around to sleeping with a few more of the beauties before his tenure was up. Wouldn't pay to completely alienate them. He opened the diary he kept at work and wrote:

Diary: November 20, 1969

I just saw Mark and Shelly. It rolls off your tongue like it's one word, Marknshelly. It strikes me that what galls me most at this moment is not that Mark got my job but that he got her.

I really liked her, and the fact that she was a Negro attracted me in an odd sort of way. She was black and there was a part of me which thought I could overcome that.

We walked together that chilly October night, and all I could think of was wanting to warm her in my arms. When the streetlights illuminated her eyes, I could have sworn she wanted to be with me too. I convinced her to let me into the Jones' apartment where she was staying. It was what I would have expected from the plain-and-unusually-dull Bob (one of the copy editors at Dobbs, Schultz & Brandon) and his wife. Everything in order, dishes laid out in a perpetual state of readiness, like the Jones' were always expecting someone. Before I could get the full lay of the land, Mark was there knocking at the door, like he knew we'd be coming.

Shelly opened the door and backed up. "What do you want?" she snorted placing her hand near her nose. Apparently, he stank. Mark looked like crap. His hair was matted, and he was barefoot. He looked like he smelled.

'Mark, old man, what brings you to us so late?' I spat. He was seething. I should have been able to predict he'd do something stupid. Bob's wife, Donna, yelled from somewhere in the back of the apartment. Shelly turned to look, and my head snapped: sucker-punched by the scrupulous Mark Schultz. My lip split and gushed blood. His rage backfired. Shelly was furious with him and all sympathy for me. I loved it.

But the blood, the sickening, sticky ooze changed everything. If I had known it would end like this, I would have avoided the whole affair: Shelly, Mark, the whole thing. Nothing was worth having **IT** come back, dominant, tormenting and controlling. All of it, back in my head.

"Mr. O'Neil." Marge was pounding on his door. "Mr. Dobbs is here to see you."

CHAPTER 3

Not Me

Twenty-three-year-old Anita Kincaid loved life. What's not to love? Her father, the most powerful man on earth, adores her: the way she looks, her dark black hair sweeping her shoulders as she turns her head, the way she moves, swift and decisive, making strides in all directions, and the way she thinks, powerful and proud. So why this distance between them? Was it her mother? She'd never thought of her as a threat before, but things were definitely changing and not for the best.

Akiko Designs was Anita's idea: from picking the location on Faired Street—with great pedestrian traffic near the apartments of the idle-rich and the business elite with lots of time and money—to picking the décor: warm, red, and gold, a Byōbu folding screen with painted big cats partially shielding a black leather chaise lounge for young lovers to sit and dream. Japanese-old-world meets American modern, the marrying of two cultures. Something her mother had chosen. Something she never would.

Anita pondered these things as she returned from her break to her "mother's" jewelry shop with a question on her mind. "Shelly, tell me how is it my father gets the idea that it's time for his wife to have some outside work and I end up being the worker? I would not have helped to make this happen if I had known I'd be the victim of my own suggestions."

"Anita," Shelly huffed, busily re-shelving several bracelets and not bothering to face her as she answered, "your father said you were floundering and that working in this shop, that you conceived, would help you to get some perspective about following through."

"Ah, yes, I remember. 'Nita, you finish the school I send you to. You study finance. You live in the U.S. where my people come from, not in Japan where your mother's people come from.' Who should have a father like this? Is your father this way? Do it my way only?"

Shelly drummed her fingers on the glass showcase filled with Anita's mother's handcrafted jewels and squashed up her nose while answering. "Anita," she swelled, as if talking to a stubborn child, "my father split from my mother when I was a baby, then my mother left me. If it wasn't for Mama Rose, I don't know what would have happened to me. I'd love to have your problem. I really would: a mother who cares too much and a father who protects too much. Let me see if I can get a grip on that . . . I can't. Anita, your parents love you, and they just want you to accomplish something. Start and —"

"I won't!" Anita pounded her fist on the glass. "Harold is coming home soon. We'll be married. Then I'll do exactly what I want."

"Anita, I had no idea." Shelly turned from the black lacquered tansu which contained an unusual mix of cleaning products, loose jewels and Anita's secret project. "You are engaged?"

"I didn't say that . . . exactly. But I will marry Harold. I want it and so does he."

"I hope you'll be happy."

"Why would I not?" Anita wanted to curse Shelly. She walked across the store to do just that when she spied him. "Shelly," she rasped, "he's on his way. You'd think he'd have something better to do than to hang around here all the time. Does he have any family? Did you know he was here on the first of the year? I've made a name for him, *Mr. Green eyes.*"

"Not 'Clint Eastwood'?" Shelly winked.

"The cowboy?"

"The actor. Didn't you hear those girls in here the other day talking about the cute lines at the corner of his eyes? 'Just like Clint,' that lanky woman said nearly falling over him. I don't know a woman who doesn't think he's handsome."

"Handsome? I find those eyes eerie, so very green." Anita shuddered and rubbed up and down her arms, "You know, Shelly, I don't prefer white men."

"What an odd thing to say, your father is white."

"So, I didn't pick him my mother did—"

"And what about Harold, he's not white?" Shelly questioned as she walked toward the back room.

"Oh no, Haruto is his given name. My Haruto is from Japan, my real home."

"Anita, with you being mixed, isn't America your home too?" She returned jangling a wristlet-sized ring of clattering keys.

"Shush, he's coming."

"Miss Kincaid, Miss Schultz."

Anita tried to see what was so wonderful about Cameron O'Neil. His teeth were perfectly white, and his clothes fit like a mannequin. Shelly was married with a young child, yet she still seemed a bit dazzled by him. Oh well, there was no accounting for some people's taste.

"That's Mrs. to you, Cameron. What has brought you to our store today?" Shelly was stern but kind.

Anita had the feeling Shelly was working her way up to sharing the gospel with him as she had done with her mother, Akiko.

"The same thing that brings me every day. Your winning smile, of course and our daily repartee concerning things, which you so aptly point out, I have no understanding of: the supernatural and other ethereal matters."

Shelly shook her head and busied herself rearranging rings in the showcase. "How do you manage to be here for hours and keep up with your work at the agency?" Shelly questioned.

"You mean the work I do for your husband?" Cameron sniped. "I could do that job with one arm tied behind my back, besides the B & D job has lost its appeal since it added the 'S,' no offense."

"None taken, Cameron, if you could offend me you would have done it long ago."

"Shelly, whatever do you mean—"

"Mr. O'Neil." Anita stamped her foot. "You must know that when you insult her husband you insult her."

"Shelly, I honestly never meant—"

"Mr. Cameron, please—" Anita continued, watching him remove his suit coat and drape it over his arm.

"I believe you, Cameron," Shelly started, "but I'm afraid the time has come for you to stop insulting my husband. The two of us really are one."

"Sounds perfectly arcane, but at your request." Cameron gave Shelly one of his signature bows.

"Look at the time," Shelly said peering up at the black lacquered clock, "gotta get the baby. Mama Rose has an errand tonight. You have to close, Anita. Remember?" She hurried, pushing the large gaggle of keys in Anita's direction.

"Sure, why not. Now even you think I'm your disposal."

Cameron smiled. "That's *at*, at your disposal."

"What?" Anita snapped. "Things will change when, when..." Shelly pulled her wool coat off the metal tree and was out the door, "...I don't like to be here alone!" Anita yelled after her.

"I'll stay with you." Cameron leaned toward her, flashing his wicked smile.

"Thank you," she heard her voice squeak, "Mr. O'Neil."

"I liked Mr. Cameron better." He was reaching for her hand.

"Sure, Mr. O'Neil," she rushed, pushing the polishing cloth toward him. "You can help me wipe this, then put the Passion Collection away."

"The Passion Collection, eh.. ?" The corner of his lip tilted slightly.

"Mr. O'Neil," she smirked, "you really are what they say, aren't you?"

CHAPTER 4

The Turning Tide

A week ago —as was becoming his habit—he had come to annoy Mark by hitting on his lovely, divertingly entertaining, black wife, Shelly. She was one of the prettiest women he knew, and because of her, he had entertained the idea of dating outside his race. He had thought Mark was a fool to marry her though. In the ad business image was everything, and agents had been shut out for lesser offenses. But in Shelly's case...

Hmm, Cameron recognized he was treading on dangerous ground. He had managed to avoid Mark most days and he certainly was not afraid, but the man had a baby, and if a man loved his kid, he'd do what he could to protect him. At least that's what he should do.

Besides, since staying to help close the store, something had happened. Something had changed. He had come every day for a week to let Shelly leave and help Anita. Anita, not Shelly, commanded his attention these days.

Shelly had pitied him. Thought he needed saving. She wasn't obnoxious, but he could see through her kindness and soft touch. He could plainly see what she was trying to do. But there would be no conning a con. Anyway none of that mattered. His new reason for visiting this shop was Anita.

This little half and half, Japanese-white girl had done everything in her power to offend. She rebuffed him and insulted him. Women never treated him like this—at least not until after he was done with them. But Anita also made him laugh. Their encounters were like finding that proverbial four-leaf clover, a thing simultaneously mundane and beautiful. He smiled, pulling on the ornamental brass handle to Akiko Designs. So what if he left Dobbs, Schultz & Brandon an hour early, with no scheduled appointments; they didn't seem to notice and he no longer cared if they did.

When he entered the store everything looked as if he were seeing it for the first time. The counters were wiped to a glistening gleam, showing off the handcrafted works of Akiko Kincaid: the talented, understated wife of business mogul, Chuck Kincaid, owner of Kincaid International Import-Export, Kincaid Fine Jewelry, and numerous other ventures.

It was obvious that his demure wife expressed herself in every bauble. Akiko's azure blues sang of a home long forgotten, of waters flowing over sea-washed stone and of majestic shrines erected to ancient deities. Asia called to him from the black and red paneled screen with their golden tigers' eyes; he halted in step and breath. What was he to encounter today, trick or treat? His mind measured the question as the two women, Akiko's daughter, Anita, and Mark's wife, Shelly, emerged from the red-cloaked back room.

"Cameron, how nice: you're here."

Cameron stared blankly. No one stood between him and Anita. In the corner a young couple huddled, perhaps contemplating the fine diamond-jade ring set, housed there. Could she be talking to him? Even when she tolerated him she wasn't gracious. Surely she was speaking to someone else and using his name.

"Miss Kincaid, or shall we both be on a first name basis?" he answered finally, admiring the red and black Oriental-inspired, tight-fitting dress she wore.

"Excuse me, Miss," a graying woman emerged from nowhere, looking to all the world as if she was working hard at emanating an air of sophistication. "Can you tell me how much this bracelet with the amber stones is?"

"Just one minute," Anita replied staring directly into his eyes.

"If you could just tell me the price—"

"And, if you could just wait your turn," Anita snapped, turning to give the woman her full attention and venom. "Are you sure you're in the right place? We don't have anything less than fifty dollars."

"Well I... I..." The old woman twitched, fumbled with her yellowing neck scarf, marshaled what dignity she could and marched to the door.

Cameron could hardly tell what he was feeling. Something between irritation and disappointment fought for dominance. For some reason he wanted Anita to be better than this. Even he could sympathize with the less fortunate.

"That, Dear Anita," he eked out slowly, "was beneath you."

"I... I don't know what you mean, Cameron."

"And this too is a pity." Cameron pulled his collar up against the shrill wind and followed the elderly woman's path to the doorway.

Shelly noticed Anita's porcelain-like face contort.

"Do you understand what just happened? I don't understand . . ," Anita said scurrying across the tongue and groove floor, her dark hair flapping in the wind as she pushed on the entry door. "I thought he worshiped my steps. I had no idea he could be, would be, such a…a…stick in the mud." She was saying this as she stuck her head out looking both left and right. "This is very confusing." She turned to Shelly. "Extremely, dis… discerting."

"*Disconcerting*, you mean disconcerting."

"Yes, of course I do." Her hands flew to her narrow hips. "The very time I decide to be nice to him; to show him a little mercy, he does this to me." Her red lips were in a pout as her shiny black pump thumped an angry tune on the hard wood floor.

"What?" Shelly questioned squinting in her direction.

"Don't play stupid with me, Shelly." Anita walked toward her, pointing, "You know very well what. He judged me. He just stood there and told me, with no words, that he was disappointed. Who is he to be disappointed, him of all people?"

Who indeed, Shelly mused. The Cameron she knew had doubled his efforts at being aloof in matters such as these. What could make him take note of Anita's bad behavior, especially toward someone who, to him, could not matter in the least and what about the consequences of interfering? He might have ruined his chances with Anita, even if his interest was, in all probability, just physical.

"Anita, what a lovely piece," Shelly said picking up the purple and red ornate bracelet from the felt lined box Anita left lying on the glass counter. Anita could see that Shelly had been trying extra hard to cheer her up since the day Cameron had snubbed her and had not bothered to return and explain himself. She wasn't sure why Shelly thought that anything Cameron did could bother her. She really didn't care.

"These jewels are magnificent." Shelly continued, twirling the thick bracelet between her thumb and forefinger and examining the small diamonds surrounding the ruby with her magnifying glass. "What are you going to do with it?"

"I'm going to add it to our collection of course." *What else would I be doing with it?*

"You must be joking. It's much too extravagant. It doesn't fit with anything your mother has created."

"So we can't do something different, something new? Why does it always have to be the old way, the same? I'm so tired of doing things their way."

"Anita, what is this really about?"

"Shelly, have you ever been in love?"

Shelly's nose crinkled as she walked around the opposite side of the counter still examining the heavy bracelet. "Has it been that long? Am I some old married woman?"

"Oh Shelly, I know you were in love. Are. Are in love, with Mark."

"Anita, you're in love. With Haruto, remember?"

Anita sat up straight on a stool behind the counter and stared off into the distance. "We call him Harold here in America." She smoothed her dress, clutched her knees and leaned forward. "I met him in my country. He works for Kincaid Enterprises." Her words came faster, "My dad trusts him with his whole Japanese branch, but with his daughter, his precious daughter, Haruto cannot be trusted. And I. . . I love him. . ." She stopped in mid-sentence as if a contrary thought had interrupted her. She shook her head, "Can't my father even trust me, my heart? What about what I want? We're selling the bracelet with the collection and that's that."

"Well, if you can find someone who comes into this store expecting to buy one of your mom's pieces and buys that instead, then why not. And, Anita, I really hope you and your true love are united after all."

CHAPTER 5

The Deal

Anita Kincaid, Anita Kincaid, he kind of hummed it on his way to her mother's jewelry store. Irritating Mark was not his incentive for going to Akiko's today. It was Anita. He hadn't planned on her. This fierce little woman was like a splinter under his nail. It was irritating, but it let him know he was alive.

He had walked the eight blocks from his apartment thinking about Mrs. Mimier for the last two. Anita had treated her badly. She was a poor woman with an unexpected severance package who had been retired. Early.

Mrs. Mimier's tears flowed liberally when she relayed that piece of information. "I can still type, Mr. O'Neil. My filing skills are impeccable, and I didn't do anything wrong." His gut wrenched when she told him this. He had retired an old or unattractive secretary or two, himself. With the dollar bills fresh in her gnarled hands she wandered into Akiko's to buy her daughter something she had never been able to buy her before, a genuine gem. He didn't know what made him go after her. But he was glad he did. She was a nice lady, and she told him he had a good heart. He didn't remember ever being told that. He took her number saying, "I know some people. I bet we can get you working again in no time." She kissed his cheek. It felt good.

He quickened his pace. He wanted to get to Anita. He wanted to give her a chance to prove she was better than she showed with Mrs. Mimier. This couldn't be who she really was. He wanted to believe that she was better. He couldn't remember the last time something like this was important to him.

He had arrived. 12 Faired Street, Akiko Designs' door lay two steps away. Deep breath.

"Ladies, Prince Charming alights." He was pulling the carved glass door open when he noticed Anita drying her eyes. "Were you crying, Miss Kincaid?" His chest tightened. "Can I be of assistance?"

"Only if you are willing to buy these rather clunky earrings." She shoved the large gem monstrosities across the glass and over the tastefully delicate pieces encased beneath the counter. "Or the matching bracelet," she sighed. There were no tears in her eyes, but distress was etched over her pretty face.

"And how, may I ask, would this help you?" He pulled a handkerchief from his jacket pocket as an offering.

"Thank you." She pushed out her lower lip while taking the cloth from his hand. "It's this way. If I sell these pieces of the Passion Collection, it might prove to Shelly that I have some sense for this business that my mother and I conceived. And it might prove to my parents that I can make some decisions that create the desired outcome. Never mind, I'm in your way. You came to flirt with Shelly or to tell me what a bad person I am."

So she had noticed. "I'm leaving Shelly to her husband." He propped his elbows on the counter. "And I think I'd like to do something to improve your unflattering opinion of me."

"You care what I think of you?" Her dusty black eyes were carrying him away.

"I'll buy them," he said lifting and examining the odd red and purple jewels, surrounded by a number of small diamonds and laced through with black velvet. "What will they set me back? Five, six hundred…"

"Thousand, two…The diamonds are of good quality even though they are small. Don't worry, Mr. O'Neil, I won't hold you to it."

"Miss Kincaid, you mistake me. I could never leave you in distress." *And for the life of me I don't know why.* "I'll purchase them. Can you sell them on installments?" He half hoped she could not, would not. Let's forget this whole thing, he wanted to say. He survived on wise financial decisions and thrift, not chivalry. Besides, he was a cad and every bad thing that was said about him was true, yet he wanted to keep his word to her. **Your word? Huh! Your entire life is a lie. You are no good and you know it.**

"Mr. O'Neil." He felt someone close to him. "Mr. O'Neil, are you there?" She was waving her delicate hand before his eyes.

"What hum... yes, yes, what was I saying?" It was happening again, but he could control it.

"Nothing." She looked puzzled. "I was saying that I will allow it on installments. When do you think you will have it paid in full? I'd like to report my success to my mother and father. They need to know that I have the ability to do something on my own."

"Yes, well, is six months a reasonable amount of time?"

"Yes, yes, how can I repay you, Mr. Cameron?" She was fluttering her thick black lashes. "This is too wonderful. You can't know what this means to me. Getting my parents to trust my judgment is very necessary. If they can see that I make good decisions, well you don't know how you've helped me. What can

I do for you? There must be something to repay this kindness. I know you didn't come in here for this, and I'm starting to feel guilty." She held his hands in hers.

"Don't. I wasn't planning on buying anything today, but I can certainly make use of such fine jewelry. And you can do me the great favor of having lunch with me… say seven?"

"Lunch at 7:00?" She withdrew her hands from his. "That makes no sense. Morning or night?"

"You mistake me, Miss Anita. I mean seven lunches. It's the least you can do to help me avoid looking obvious and pathetic. And it will give Mrs. Schultz time to be free of my prying eyes."

"Mr. O'Neil, I cannot have lunch with you seven times. Haruto…um-um how would that look? We are not dating. But I am more than willing to have lunch with you once or even twice if it will help you in some way. That's the least I can do."

"Once or twice is hardly enough to satisfy my need for diversion, but I will settle for three."

"If this will satisfy you than I will submit."

"Submit. That's not very romantic, but I'll take it. Our first date is a week from today. Deal?"

"Yes, I said I would."

"Until then, *mi amour.*" With that Cameron spun on his heel, gave a sly smile, and headed for the door.

"I think his eyes were twinkling," Shelly hummed from the other side of the store.

"Why do I feel I've just made a deal with the devil?" Anita whispered, careful to make sure Cameron was really gone.

Andy's was a little burger joint tucked away in an old north-side residential neighborhood. Because Cameron was afraid his sporty Jaguar would be an iffy venture given the prediction of icy roads, he drove Marge's borrowed '67 Ambassador. As he and Anita walked the two blocks from where he parked the car, he started to feel guilty. His idea was to show her the neighborhood, which could best be done on foot. Even though it was sunny and unseasonably warm for January it was still cold. He took off his overcoat and draped it over her shoulders. She looked like a mythical creature: short and shrouded, his long coat sweeping the ground on her small body. She smiled up at him. He felt warm.

"One of my friends brought me to this neighborhood when I was a teen," Cameron answered to her unasked question. His hands were deep in his pockets, and a thick scarf was double wrapped around his neck.

"What?" he asked as she stared, some other question etched on her forehead.

"The sun is very bright. Is that why you do it?"

"Do what?" He could feel the smile crossing his lips.

"Wear them. You wear sunglasses in winter. I don't know anyone who does that."

"Oh that." He took the glasses off and looked down at her. "Better?"

"Oh I don't care." She smiled.

He started to put them on again. She grabbed his hand and tugged before he could.

"Wait, I change my mind. I can see those lines that Shelly talked about. The one's circling your eyes like the sun's beams. You make your own green suns, two of them," she laughed. "I forbid you to put those monstrous glasses back on."

"Ever again?"

"Ever again."

He crumpled the wire rims in his hand and tossed them away. "Now what?"

"Continue..."

"Continue?" He felt off balance. A new kind of strange.

"Your story."

"My story. Yes this neighborhood, it's a simple area, but I like it in a way that's hard to explain."

"Let me see if I can figure it out," Anita teased. "Possible clients?"

He looked down to see if she was serious.

"I'm teasing, Mr. O'Neil."

Despite his best efforts, his smile relaxed into a straight line.

Anita knew what he wanted, and he had purchased those awful earrings with that bulky bracelet.

"Cameron." He seemed distant. "Cameron," she said it louder, "try to put into words why you like this place?"

"Okay." He stopped wide-legged and arms extended in front of a single story yellow brick house surrounded by a low white picket fence. "This house belonged to Donny Dancer."

She sighed and folded her arms across her chest.

"I'm not joking. Donny Dancer was my first friend when I moved to Chicago, and he lived here with his two sisters." He stretched out his arms toward the enormous leafless trees in the yard. "Their names were Diana and Dana." He beamed as if savoring a memory. "When the sun went down, Donny's father, Donny Sr., would grab Donna, his wife, like this." Why had she looked up into his eyes? He acted like it was an invitation. He grabbed her by the hand and put his free arm around her waist. They twirled one way and then the other.

Anita's feet left the ground literally and she wished, when he put her down, that he had whirled her two more times.

"I loved this house." He smiled down at her, and they walked a couple of houses more, close together.

Her arm rubbed against his and even through her coat and his, she felt him. If only there wasn't all this stuff between us, she thought, then visibly shook herself.

"Ah, here we are, this is the home of the LaFeats. The mother is a kind woman who makes warm dinners and greets her five children with a smile when they run through that front door." He pointed over her head and kind of let his arm drape her shoulder as he brought it back down. "The father is Edward. He's a soft-spoken man who works nine to five and never lets the company give him overtime. He insists on being home to sit at his oak dining table with the silver chain light fixture hanging overhead. There is a round glass vase with yellow daisies sitting in the middle. They are having beef stew."

Anita knew Cameron was talking about a home he wished he had or used to have. She didn't have the heart to ask him which. Her heart thumped heavily as they left that house with its porch swing and handmade mailbox.

"You know, Anita, you are a good listener. I don't understand why some young upstart hasn't offered for your hand and whisked you off to places exotic."

"Mr. —" she started.

He gave her a look.

"Cameron," she corrected.

"I can't imagine. . ," he mused, no longer waiting for or wanting an answer.

That was okay with Anita. For some reason, she no longer wanted to give him an answer.

They walked on. The aroma of sizzling onions and fried burgers escaped to meet them as a young couple exited the small diner. "Andy's, yes?"

"Yes, and this brings me to a very unpleasant revelation. This is our third lunch, but I've really enjoyed our time together. Do you think we could do it again?"

Anita felt her stomach tumble, one flop then another. "I don't know, Cameron, you too are easy to talk with. I can't explain it. It is perhaps not proper."

"Anita, you are not engaged, and I certainly am not. I don't see what is not proper about it. And besides, I have a confession, when I am with you I feel better, a kind of ease. You probably don't have a clue what that means, but when I'm with you I forget."

"Is it good to forget?"

"It is when all you remember is… You know what, never mind all that. Let's talk about you."

"Me?"

"Yes, you. For three dates you have given ear to the droning of the loneliest man on the planet. Your turn, talk."

The metal door screeched as he pulled it open. Andy's was small, crowded and dingy. She didn't care. For some reason it looked like a palace to her. "You want to hear about me?"

"I do. Just for today pretend I am someone you can trust and tell me your deepest desires."

"Be careful what you ask for, Mr. Cameron, you might just get it."

"Anita, if you can just call me Cameron, we will be halfway there."

"Well, I want… I want what everyone wants."

Cameron nodded and peered directly at her. His ocean-green eyes sparkled and were making her woozy.

"I want," she took a steadying breath, "to be accepted. I want to be appreciated, and I want respect."

"That was unexpected."

"You don't like my answer, then."

"It's a fine answer, just not very romantic."

"Must every woman be romantic? What does that get for you? Besides if I had what I wanted my love would follow."

"That's, 'love would follow.'" He pulled a chair out for her to sit down. "You said, 'my' love would follow.'"

"Perhaps that is what I meant. My English falters when I am nervous."

"I'd wager you are never nervous," Cameron said, seating himself, " but you are correct, your English did falter, just this one time."

Anita watched as he rested his chin on his hand, and in the privacy of her thoughts she admitted that his blond hair and green eyes did not offend her.

And what do you want, Cameron? He parked the green Ambassador on the street in front of his apartment, pushed open the cracked glass door on the ground floor of his neglected building and headed up the stairs wishing Anita had asked him the question. Because for some reason he felt he would have answered, "I want to feel free. I want someone to look past my appearance and see what I might be. I want someone to love me not because of what I do and despite of what I've done. I want to know that someone knows me and loves me anyway. Is there such a thing, such a state of being? Can my conscience be calm and not some intrusive outside force that barks at me? Can I just feel clean and accepted?" For some reason he felt he would have been honest with Anita, for some reason he felt he might be … crazy. Exactly. No one fell in love after a few lunches and months of near proximity, absolutely no one, especially not the reluctant Mr. O'Neil. Except he didn't feel so reluctant these days… Lately he had been feeling downright "luctant," if there was such a word.

He who judged everyone, but was judged of none, was allowing himself to be vulnerable. *I hardly recognize myself,* he thought as he walked briskly down the street, the wind stinging his face. *What has Anita done to me? No one has been to my apartment. Not a man, not a woman, no one has been to my home. Wait, there was that one time with Amanda. She doesn't count.* He rubbed his hands together and stuck them in his pockets. *I'm not sure what she is. And if she has any feelings, I've never seen them. The way she treated Marge. The cutthroat underhanded…*

Marge who never hurt anyone, he hissed, watching his breath on the air. Who was he becoming? Who was he to talk? He was conveniently cold when women hinted at coming to his place after a date. His warmth returned when the lady changed her mind and invited him to her place or when his invitation to join him at a hotel was accepted. These days most women, who weren't slow, knew where a date with him would end and few ever questioned him twice.

And he wasn't exactly a man's man, seeing how most men either feared or despised him. So what was it about Anita? She was different. He wanted her to know him and maybe even to accept him. Anita asked questions, not just the, "Where you from?" type, but "Did you enjoy living there? Did that make you sad? How will you know when you've got what you're looking for?" For some reason he really liked when she asked him that. Her interest was genuine. Anyway, he hoped it was. The truth was he was just weary. One too many games, one too many grabs for power. The whole Shelly and Mark thing had soured him. He was never really the same after the night Mark bloodied his mouth. The torment returned, yes. But something else was in play, had to be, or he would have gone mad by now.

Ah, Nettie Anne's: the bright green awning had almost escaped his notice, he was so preoccupied with his thoughts. He made a sharp turn into the unassuming eatery to pick up his favorite chicken dish.

It was smothered with green peppers and onions. He would also get some margarine-soaked baked potatoes, corn, sautéed green beans and a couple after-dinner Danishes. He thought he was a fair cook, but to be honest the theory had never been tested. After all, who had eaten his cooking but him? Because he liked it didn't mean anyone else would, and he wanted Anita to like it. He had only to decide if he'd take credit for cooking or give Nettie Anne her due. No, that was the old Cameron. He'd tell Anita the truth, especially if she didn't care for it. He smiled. There was still plenty of the old him left.

CHAPTER 6

Broken Promises

A kiko Designs, her mother's signature venture, was a success. Anita thought as she held the door open for Shelly as they arrived for work. *People loved Mrs. Akiko Kincaid's striking but modest creations, a seeming contradiction that brought women in by the dozens, many pulling their lovers along.*

Irritation pricked Anita. Of all the places Shelly could employ her management skills, why did it have to be here? Most days they did the same work, but when Shelly felt like it, she pulled rank, running off anytime she wanted to be with her new baby. Why didn't she just quit? Surely her child was more important than the promise she had made to someone else's mother.

"Mama Rose loves to spend time with L.J." was always her excuse. Apparently Shelly liked ruling over her more than being with her own child. And wouldn't she like to spend more time with her giant husband who she was always bragging about?

What was Mark? Nothing compared to the man she loved, her Haruto. Her man was a Japanese National, dark and certain. In their home country, he was a shrewd businessman: so much promise. When her father introduced her to him she fell instantly in love. She loved his power, the way he commanded men, causing them to immediately line up. She knew he could match her father and someday he would have a dynasty of his own. She hadn't spent a whole week with him before she knew he was the man for her. When she told her father how she felt he simply said, "We will see." She was furious. "See what?" she demanded. "You think I don't know what I want? I want Haruto."

"You are impetuous, Anita. This is not a new dress or change of school. Haruto is spineless in the worst way, a worm who wiggles his way into any crack to get ahead in his business dealings. I'm not sure that does not extend to his personal affairs, to you." He pointed in her direction, "I've given you everything you want, but I cannot give you this."

For as long as Anita could remember, her father had never refused her one thing, and the one time when it mattered the most, he decided to be stingy. He was afraid that Haruto would be more attached to her than to his work, and maybe just maybe, he'd leave Kincaid Enterprises and run away with her. When she told her father that, he laughed. Said he could see that he had not raised her well, that she had too much time on her hands. Time she spent summoning up imaginary relationships. "It's my job, daughter, to save you from yourself." He was at his easel, wearing a traditional navy blue *yukata* and painting landscapes. "Father, you married a Japanese woman and you wear our clothing more often than you wear American clothes. I have more right to my homeland than you do. You are white."

His grin was jarring, "Daughter, are you a racist? I love your mother, and I love Japan." Chuck Kincaid took a step down off his wooden platform admiring his handiwork. "If I thought you truly loved Japan, I'd let you live there. If I thought you truly loved Harold, I'd let you marry him. Though I don't think you could ever be happy with him. You see, to please me, he'd let you abuse him totally, and you could never respect a man you could abuse."

Then there was that faithful night of her father's dinner party. He had summoned the Brandon & Dobbs executives to his home to see if they were worthy of his precious ad dollars. They, she and Shelly, had convinced her mother to sell her handcrafted jewelry. But mother was too shy to actually face the people in the shop, so her father seized the opportunity to put his wayward child in a position to learn some responsibility. She was no fool; this job was to beat the rebellion out of her, bring her to her senses, and—she thought—for her father to gain a small bit of retribution. She had had the audacity to tell Haruto how she felt. He was thrilled and said he welcomed the opportunity to become part of the Kincaid family. He would offer for her hand when he returned to the States. Her father said "it" would never happen. Did he mean Haruto offering for her or simply him refusing permission? Whatever he meant, she had become estranged from him. For the first time in her life, she was not close to her father, and he didn't miss her. Her mother didn't weigh in. That was okay. Anita didn't really care what she thought. She was too quiet, always doing what he wanted, never insisting on her own way. Anita would never be like her, never.

"Banished, banished," Anita muttered as she pulled open the door to Akiko Designs where her shy mother should be. Shelly, her would-be friend and co-worker pranced forward wearing a burnt orange dress and an eerily cheerful smile. "How was your break, Anita? Are you feeling better?"

"I wasn't feeling bad, Shelly. I simply hate this dungeon. Perhaps if I was not a 'shiftless do-nothing' it would be I who manages and you who takes the orders."

"That's not fair, Anita. Yes, Mr. Kincaid gave me managerial responsibility, but that's only until you know what you want to do."

"What I want to do, Shelly, is not to be working here Monday, Tuesday, Wednesday, and Saturday. Thank God my mother is insisting that the store be closed on Sundays. She says she doesn't care what Sears or any other company does. Akiko's will never be open on Sunday. I guess I have to thank you for that too."

"Your mother wanted to attend—"

"Church, yes, I know, and I suppose that would matter if she actually worked here selling HER stuff."

"Sorry to see you so dissatisfied. But cheer up! Cameron will be here soon. Seems he amuses you." Shelly sauntered to the rear of the store.

Cameron O'Neil, Anita thought. He had come at first to annoy his rival, Shelly's husband, Mark. *Mark could not guard his precious wife here*, Anita imagined Cameron saying. But over the past few months, Cameron O'Neil had taken an interest in her; she was not at all sure why.

Harold had been out of the country, so indulging Cameron could harm no one. And Cameron had his good points; his wit and unusual green eyes grew on you. Making her father aware that they had had a date or two was an added benefit. Daddy hated the man.

"So you are going out with Cameron tonight," Shelly's delight-filled voice echoed from where she had waltzed to dust and pick up, interrupting Anita's thoughts. Anita did not respond. Shelly craned her neck around the Byōbu, her smile turning into a straight line. "That wasn't a question for you to think about. It was a confirmation of what I assumed was a fact. Cameron's only been by here two times asking why you weren't in yet."

"No," Anita said flatly.

"No what?"

"No, I am not going out with Mr. O'Neil tonight. I have other plans."

"Anita, you can't."

"Oh but I can, Haruto is coming home tonight, and I will have time for only him. You will tell Cameron for me."

"I will not. He'll be... well I think he'll be heartbroken."

"Yes, exactly. You think. Even you know he is not a man of deep feeling and emotion. He will no sooner care that I have broken a date than if a client had to change an appointment, and you and I both know he can have another date with the wink of an eye. No, my Haruto is home, and I will not have any more time for Cameron." Anita grabbed her finely designed broad-collared coat and lurched toward the door. "Please tell him for me."

Shelly stood with her hands on her hips and her mouth open wide. My, how the tide had turned. Anita, who Shelly once admired, was turning into a selfish, overly indulged brat. And unless she missed her guess, the impenetrable Cameron O'Neil was about to hit a brick wall capable of breaking him.

"Not here?" Cameron entered Akiko Designs laying a heavy paper bag on the glass counter while rushing to the back of the store as if not believing his own words. "She has unfortunately forgotten our plans then." He stopped in mid-stride. Shelly shuddered noting his slightly bowed shoulders and broken tone. "No matter. I have work to do. Perhaps you and Schultz would like a duty free meal?"

Shelly was about to shake her head "no" when her stomach gurgled from the scent of fresh pastry.

"Come on, Shelly, it's great stuff. Home cooking without the dirty dishes." A wave of emotion gripped her. She knew Cameron as well as he allowed himself to be known, and she just knew this was a stretch for the man. Either he was planning a picnic, which wasn't likely given the weather, or he was taking Anita home. This was a different Cameron from the one they all thought they knew. She hoped Anita's thoughtlessness would not damage Cameron more than he already was.

"O'Neil." Shelly's husband barreled into the shop bristling from the wind and uncovering the bouncing baby boy he held in his arms.

"Schultz," Cameron snapped back.

"Bothering Shelly again?" he was saying as he handed Shelly their child and removed his own coat.

"No...actually just dropping off your dinner," Cameron spouted, doing his best imitation of a western barkeep, sliding the large bag over the glass counter.

Mark stopped the bag before it tipped over the edge. "That sounds…. nice."

"You sound surprised. Like someone of my ilk is hardly capable of an unselfish act."

Mark stood, stunned.

"Enjoy your wife and child, Shultz." Cameron marched to the door and pushed it open. "You're a lucky man." The wind blew in, Cameron walked out.

With his hand still resting on the paper shopping bag and mouth agape, Mark stared after Cameron.

"What's wrong, Hon?" Shelly quipped, kissing her baby's bronze cheeks.

Mark scratched his head. "Cameron alright? When I was speaking with him—"

"Speaking with him? How about sparring with him?" she questioned over her baby's head while his little hand reached toward the buttons down the front of her dress.

"That's just it. He seemed different, subdued. How's he seem to you?"

"No… you are not worried about Cameron?" Shelly handed her little son to her husband and tugged on the heavy metal zip of his snowsuit to free him.

"Rumor is he's going to quit the firm," Mark continued absently.

"You mean Dobbs, Schultz & Brandon, is no longer in danger of being toppled from within?"

"I guess not." Mark lifted the squiggling infant from his outerwear and tossed him gently in the air.

"What'd the mean man bring us to eat? Hope it's not poison." He sniffed the air. "Sure smells good."

"Yes it does. Listen, Honey, I know Cameron's not your favorite person. But he's different, searching…"

"Here it comes."

"What? You think he's not worthy. Remember—"

"I know, I know." Mark raised his hand to silence his wife. "The Lord came for us all."

"Yes. I wonder if Cameron is ready? I think I'll give him a call."

"'The' call?"

"Yes, 'the' call. I wonder if he'd prefer the 10:00 or the 12:30 service?" She drummed her slender fingers on the glass showcase.

"Does it matter? Don't they both kind of blend in together?"

Squinting and reaching for her baby, Shelly turned her back on her handsome husband. He reached around hugging both her and the baby from behind. She smiled despite herself. He had decided to leave her to the Lord's work.

Cameron flopped down on his unforgivingly hard couch and did something he had never done. He bit his lip till it bled and when the voice came, he didn't care, he didn't resist. He let his head drop back and the accusations begin.

What are you thinking? Anita can't love you. You will never be more than the philanderer you are. You will never change. Anita knows it and so do you. Running to God won't help. Give up, just like her. Give up.

It hurt badly this time. Not his lip, but the endless droning, the lack of empathy, the unrelenting oppressiveness of **IT**. "Shut up!" he shouted, but to whom? He was the only one in the room. He pressed his palms to his head. It will all go away he thought, the tightening in his chest. It will all go away, the feeling that his mind would explode. It will all go away, that longing for something else. It will all go away. Yes, even his desire for her. Within the week, he'd be back to himself, and Anita would be no more than a bad memory.

CHAPTER 7

Higher Ground

He was here. Mt. Prospect. This typical church building and largely Afro-American congregation had become part of his weekly routine. He was early. People were still getting seated. Some he recognized from the last three weeks. There were also those he had not seen before. He smiled, wondering how many Shelly was responsible for. She had invited him, but something else had drawn him. He spotted a seat close to the door and started up the aisle.

"GIVE UP, GOD HATES YOU." Before he could reach his seat, the attack began. *Not now.* Cameron hurried to the washroom to sequester himself there until **IT** passed. "HE HATED YOUR MOTHER. WHY ARE YOU HERE ANYWAY? NOBODY WANTS YOU. GIVE UP!" Then came the incessant, unrelenting stream of curses. Cursing Him. Cameron had no control, none at all.

"Stop!"

"Brother Cameron, are you okay in there?"

"Yes, I'm fine." Cameron jerked his head, trying to quiet **IT**.

Before it all went wrong, he had believed in God. But when his dad left... he knew no God would take a child's mother and father. It was after the blood that the curses came. And if God could hear thoughts, He could have no use for a man who could think such things, even if the man didn't call them up, or control them. In fact, these days, **IT**spoke whenever it wanted to, and it was aimed at the one who should have saved him in the first place. Maybe **IT** had returned to save its old friend, Cam. Yes, to save him the humiliation of seeking a God who either didn't exist or who could not care less about him. The voice that continually taunted him was just trying to tell him not to waste his time. After all, it wasn't just the thoughts; Cameron's whole life was spent cursing God in one way or another.

"Brother Cameron?"

"Yes, yes, I am all right." Cameron shook his head like a dog trying to expel water from his ear. Wednesdays at Mt. Prospect had become his refuge. On the evening that Anita stood him up, Shelly called.

"Cameron, please come to church on Sunday. I've watched you for some time. And I've been where you are."

"I doubt that," he had responded.

But when she said, "God loves you, Cameron, and he's calling you." He laughed out loud.

"Boy have you got it wrong," he'd sneered.

But when she came back with, "Wanna make a bet?" he thought this wonderfully ironic: a Christian woman betting a heathen that her God could somehow be calling him. He had to see what compelled her.

Besides, what else was he doing? He was becoming lost, drifting. Something in him was calling out for... what? God? He didn't know. He didn't have Anita anymore, and Mark was still rubbing him the wrong way. The perfect storm had brought him to this place at this time so he'd explore his motivation: find God, annoy Mark. Maybe he could do both. He felt a smile come on.

It didn't last. **LEAVE. SCREW GOD.** His palms flew to his head. He was having a moment. The intruder was back. He'd try crowding it out with a pleasant memory. Let's see... Ah, yes...

One of his happy nights: before she went into the dark and his father went away. It was like it used to be. His mother had washed the dishes and was sitting on his bed. She smiled down at him. They were waiting for his father to finish brushing his teeth. He bounced in wearing his blue and yellow pajamas. Cameron's hands were clasped against his soothing bedspread. He remembered closing his eyes, squinting hard to keep one completely closed while peeking with the other as he waited for his dad to join him. When his father knelt beside him, he looked into his kind and reassuring face. It registered neither anger nor disapproval. This man, his father, had accepted him and his mother unconditionally. They were happy then. This was the man he wanted to remember. The man who taught him the prayer they prayed many, many nights.

"Dear Lord, we are your children and we thank you for your provisions. We ask that every day be a day of service to you and your kingdom. Let your love abound in our hearts and show forth in the world. We ask nothing more; we give nothing less. Amen."

He remembered the words, but the meaning had long escaped him.

"Stomach problems, Cameron?" There was a voice he knew too well.

"It is entirely possible that my problems were brought on by some nuisance, and you might be correct in assuming your presence, perhaps even your very existence, is an…"

Irritant, you should know. Leave now! "Ummhhh!" Cameron grunted loudly in response to **ITs** intrusion.

"Can we please move?" Cameron heard Shelly state flatly.

"I'd say. Nobody wants to be on the other side of that bathroom door when it opens."

"Mark!"

"That settles it," Cameron groaned. "I've got to kill him."

In the tiny green bathroom, while combing his hair back into place and straightening his suit jacket, Cameron decided that as maddening as this exchange had been, he really didn't have time for the Schultzes. Tonight his real demons were plaguing him. Mark and Shelly were a mere annoyance.

CHAPTER 8

No Turning Back

Thundering out of the office of Dobbs, Schultz & Brandon, Cameron caught sight of himself in the glass, and he hardly recognized the man before him. He was disheveled and although he knew he'd be quitting soon, he had started to slack off in his work. It was crazy. He had long lost interest in the company, but in his own personal work? That wasn't like him. But he just didn't have the time or patience for DSB.

He walked for a couple of hours fighting Chicago's never-ending winds and being pushed to the place he'd sworn he never wanted to go again. He looked up and found himself back at the jewelry store. He guessed he was a glutton for punishment. He had become a regular at Mt. Prospect. It occupied much of his time, but thoughts of Anita still gripped him. He believed he needed the church, but he wanted her. And he saw no contradiction in the two, though both seemed still slightly out of his reach. He was becoming desperate. This was a new sensation. It had been years since he'd experienced unrequited anything. It had also been years since he had been unable to cap the voice of accusation. In fact lately **IT** threatened to swallow him daily. And he simply did not know what to do.

"Anita, fancy meeting you here," he exclaimed, striding once again across the floor and up to the counter of Akiko Designs Jewelry Store. He had decided to forgive Anita for standing him up, hardly ever being at the shop, and failing to seem interested in him at all anymore.

"I work here, Mr. O'Neil." She twisted her pretty red lips. Sad and happy appeared to war across her mouth.

"It's Cameron. I thought we were on a first name basis after sharing so much with each other." He hadn't meant to say that, but it was true. He had opened up to her with a willingness that stunned him.

"Mr. O'Neil, if you are here to see Shelly, she isn't here today."

"Anita, you wound me. I am here for only you."

"Cameron, I... I like you. You are not always as you appear, I can see that, but what are you? I don't know, and I ... I have other commitments. I cannot complicate—"

Cameron couldn't help himself. He had to touch her if for no other reason than to quiet her lovely mouth. He placed his finger on her lip, and if he didn't know she was impenetrable, he would have sworn he felt her swoon.

"Would you like to go for a walk?"

"No."

He was staring at her. "What do you want?" he whispered.

"I... I... don't know, Cam... Cam..."

"How 'bout that walk?" he said, still staring directly into her eyes. "I'll help you close this place, and you'll go for a walk with me."

"You'll help me close this place, and I'll go for a walk with you," she whispered back.

He wasn't sure what had just happened. Together they pushed the dusting cloths across the counters, pulled all the jewelry-filled, carved wooden cases from the shelves, counted money, and locked away the cash. An hour later, he was walking through the mild night air, the streetlights illuminating Anita's alabaster hand, which was locked through his arm. He wanted to thank someone. He just wasn't sure who.

"Cameron, if you dislike your job so much why don't you quit?"

He felt the tug on his arm as she appeared to read his thoughts.

"I should, shouldn't I?" He slowed his gait and pulled her arm more snuggly through his.

"Yes, anyone can tell you have what it takes to make it in the ad business: deceit and cunning."

"Ouch." He stopped at the curb by the stoplight and looked down at her. "Are those my only qualifications?"

"It's nothing to be ashamed of, Cameron." She looked away with a smirk. "There is a place for everyone in the world. You are simply fulfilling yours. Go start your own ad business. Americans love to push and shove their way to the top. As you all say, 'that's what makes America great.'"

"I don't think we put it quite that way." The light changed to green and they continued walking. "But listen, Anita, there must be other qualities a person like me, I mean, a person needs in order to be in the advertising business?"

"Yes of course. Let me think." She stopped again, stamping her toe, her hand poised under her chin. "Well, you must be smart and resourceful." There was a twinkle in her eye. "You obviously know people's weaknesses so you can make them buy."

"Are you insulting me?"

"Not at all. We all do what we must to make it. To me life is like a bowl of mixed fruit: the fruit's not trying to get out, it's just trying to survive next to the other pieces and if it's lucky, in mixing, it retains some of what makes it unique. Like the berry wants to stay red—"

"That's ridiculous." He laughed, "Go on..."

By the time Cameron walked into his narrow hallway, up his rickety stairs, and plopped down on his stiff couch, he realized that on his winsome walk with Anita, he had laughed no less than twelve times, much at his own expense. To tell the truth, half the time he didn't know if Anita was ridiculing or just poking fun. He wasn't entirely sure if she knew herself. He clasped his hands behind his head and leaned back. Anita was an odd duck, a curious mix—like her fruit bowl analogy—of naivety, adorableness, beauty, childlike-whimsy, intellect, and did he mention adorableness, with just a smidgen of cunning? He was sure now he was going to have her. He closed his eyes recalling her deep black eyes, cherry red mouth, and smooth, cool hands.

Minutes later he turned his thoughts to his new nemesis, Chuck Kincaid. He'd have to find some way to get around the father. The man was as sharp as an eagle. He owned at least three businesses that Cameron was aware of: his own jewelry store, an import/export business, an oriental furniture store specializing in Japanese novelties, and he was underwriting Akiko Designs—a venture that his wife and Schultz's wife ran. Cameron was still trying to figure out how Anita, Akiko's own daughter, got pushed out. She seemed to be no more than the hired help. He smiled; it was obvious this grated Anita's nerves.

The Brandon & Dobbs Advertising Agency—as it used to be called before that imitator Mark Schultz got his name added to the sign—had researched Chuck Kincaid, as they did all their clients, but Anita's father seemed to take excessive pleasure in being mysterious. No problem. He wasn't the one Cameron wanted to demystify.

Cameron walked to his compact bedroom and undressed. He laid his head on his pillow and with an unrepressed smile allowed himself to recall the last few moments of his outing with Anita.

Once inside the modest brick building that housed her father's in-town offices, they entered the elevator. It was late and lonely so he grabbed her hand. She did not pull away until the chime sounded for the second floor. They used her key to enter the main office complex where her father maintained a small apartment in the rear. They stood just inside the gold-plated glass doors. He looking down, she looking up. On impulse, he pulled her to his chest and held her there for several minutes. She was such a little bit of a woman—no more than a girl in stature—yet she was all woman. He could feel the *ancientness* of her soul. For a flicker, she molded to him then stiffened. He wanted to shake her, to make her love him, but there would be no shaking loose the fruit that would be her affection. As she pulled away and looked off to the side, he knew... this was going to be the hardest work he'd ever done.

Anita floated into her father's office apartment where he stayed when he was too tired to come home. It was neat and well kept. It even had a few of his signature Japanese artifacts, a Samurai sword hanging here and a bonsai tree there. It was sparsely decorated since he rarely used it. He wanted to be home where he could lord over her and her mother. Anyway, tonight it was just right. She had called home to let them know where she was and, after several minutes of grilling, her father agreed to let her alone. She just couldn't be around people tonight. She wanted to be alone with her thoughts. After changing to a pair of oversized men's pajamas, she slipped into the covers and thought back on her last few minutes with Cameron.

He had given her a long head-to-toe piercing look. It was not like the lech-look she had seen him use before. It was a thoughtful look, a longing look. It gave her the shudders. Then he turned and without speaking walked away leaving her standing next to the front desk. Fortunately, Miss Wood, her father's receptionist, was long gone and not seated to see their...*behavior.* Anita had found her hand waving an involuntary "good bye," and she could still feel Cameron's finger on her lip from when he had touched her at the shop. Upon this revelation, she twisted in the covers and pounded her pillow. This was impossible; she loved Haruto and was going to be his wife. Yet there was something about Cameron. She should tell him that she could never be his—that her love belonged to another—instead, she encouraged him. Without words or even physical suggestion, she continued to push him to the very brink of what was reasonable or responsible. The question was, why? Did she want to succumb, to let him love her? She punched the pillow again and pulled it over her face, smothering a screeching howl. Something deep down and stubborn forbade her from letting him in. And for some reason she had a feeling it wasn't the best part of her.

CHAPTER 9

First Family

It was Wednesday, Bible study night. Cameron waited just inside the church's back door. He knew Pastor Marvin would be finishing up his office work at precisely six o'clock, giving him just under a half hour before people arrived. The upper level was quiet. The brothers who were early, were in the small meeting room at the rear of the church on its lowest level. If he worked fast he could catch the pastor before someone else latched on to him. Pastor Seymour Marvin was a big, dark man originally from South Carolina. He had run Mt. Prospect for twenty years, interrupting a long line of Johnsons who founded the church. It had been Baptist until Shelly's grandmother started attending. She was a Pentecostal, and because of her the church had become some sort of mix. All Cameron knew for sure was that there was something inexplicable here which he felt from the very first time he came through the doors. He headed up the stairs.

Pastor Marvin was walking out of his office with his black suit coat strung over his right arm. He pulled the door behind him looking a bit battle-scarred.

"Hard day, Pastor?"

"Ah, Cameron, you startled me. You always sneak up on people like that?"

"I used to. Been trying to do a little better these days."

"Yes, well that's good. What brings you up to the mountain cave?" Pastor Marvin said smiling and rolling his large neck.

"Nothing much, I was just curious about something."

"A young man like yourself must be curious about a number of things." Pastor Marvin placed his palm on Cameron's back and gave a gentle nudge toward the back stairwell. "Let's go outside and catch some air."

Cameron followed the big man, who sort of wobbled from side-to-side, feeling like a little boy with his feelings hurt. "Pastor Marvin, I wanted to ask you something."

"Go ahead." The pastor was loosening the top two buttons of his starched white shirt.

"Why don't you call me Brother Cameron like you do so many of the other men?"

"Cameron, I would love to have you for my brother in Christ, but you have not made your confession, as far as I know, and you have not asked to be our brother here... Cameron, can I tell you something that has already been revealed to me? You are not the type of man who would respect or honor something that came too easily. If you are willing, good will come, and when it does you will be grateful rather than contemptuous. And, Cameron, the day you wish to be my brother, I will welcome you with open arms into our family. But at present you are just spectatin'. So let us just say, I respect your right to do that, and I love you as a fellow being on God's earth."

Cameron felt exposed, but he wasn't about to be deterred from his plan. "Pastor Marvin," he said pulling a dime-store notepad from his back pocket along with a silver pen. "I am doing some research for a psychology seminar in which I am a participant. I want to talk to someone here about faith healing. You see, I have agreed to take on discovering the underlying cause for a case study in which a young woman claimed to be healed from a form of mental illness. I've heard that Shelly Madison's grandmother has been instrumental in a number of faith healings at Mt. Prospect."

"That's true, son, but the truth is, so have I and so have a number of other saints at this church. Two of our newest members, Jake Schultz and his wife Irene, have facilitated a number of our healing services. You see, son, believing that God can heal you is often the only prerequisite for the initial healing."

"The initial healing?" Cameron's brow twitched, and his hand flew to the notepad.

"Yes," Pastor Marvin continued after giving Cameron an off glance, "the one that seems to be giving you the problem: the voices, the ailment—"

"What made you say voices?" Cameron pitched unnaturally.

"Just giving you some examples." Pastor Marvin placed his broad hand on Cameron's shoulder. "Cameron, God doesn't stop with just the symptom, which sickness of any kind mostly is. He wants to dig up the very root of the problem. Are you clear on what I'm saying?" His odd gray eyes were piercing.

But Cameron wasn't clear. If he could just get his "symptom" fixed that would be enough for him. That would validate him investing his time in this little church. All he needed was a clear head again and he'd be on his way. "Pastor Marvin, might I sit in on one of these healing services?"

"For your study?" Pastor Marvin squinted. Cameron squirmed.

"Yes, of course for my study. What other reason could I have?"

"Yes, indeed, what other reason." The pastor leaned back and removed his hand from Cameron. "You must know that God's work is not a spectacle to be studied and broken down for scientific research. So I'll have to say—"

"Pastor Marvin." Cameron's hands were planted firmly on both of pastor's shoulders. "If you knew how very im— significant this is to me. I mean to my project." He caught himself and shoved both hands into his pockets.

"Still, son…" Pastor Marvin stopped abruptly, looking slightly up. "Cameron, normally I would say, 'absolutely not.' Fortunately for you the voice that speaks to me has very little to do with what I want or think." Cameron grabbed Pastor Marvin's hand in both of his and shook it vigorously.

Cameron was early for the healing service. He stood outside the rough-hewn, gray stone Romanesque house before him. The bay windows looked out onto the street and the cement slab stairs bespoke stability. He hadn't thought he could envy Mark Schultz more; but he was wrong. This was a fine house for a fine family, from which came a fine son. Schultz led a charmed life, probably had never experienced a hungry day in his life or a day when he had to wonder where he'd lay his head next. Cameron cursed under his breath and strode up the fearful stairs.

A man, appearing to be about twenty, opened the door before Cameron could ring the bell or knock. "Hello," he said with a wide smile and extending his hand toward Cameron. A slender black man whom Cameron had seen at church walked in behind him. The first man told them to make themselves at home. "Sister Schultz will be ready shortly," he continued.

Cameron held his notepad and pen at the ready in case anyone made the mistake of thinking he was there to involve himself in the meeting. Chairs were arranged in a circle, and he had begun to fiddle nervously with his tie, looking for anyone who looked like they could be Mark's mother or father. He was leaning against the wall and was beginning to feel like a complete outcast, standing while everyone else was seated. He was sure he looked like one too. In this room, which could comfortably seat eight to ten people, sat thirteen squeezed shoulder to shoulder. And just when he thought he could not be more uncomfortable, in walked his nemesis, Mark Schultz.

"O'Neil, what can you possibly be doing here?"

"Research."

"Research? The Bradley seminar on psychological influences and persuasion? Are you even part of that? It doesn't matter. I'm sorry, brother, but I am not about to let you ridicule my church and beliefs to bolster your ego or your pedigree."

"That's clever, Schultz. Did you write that or did your little wife? Are you still relying on her to pull you out of advertising malaise?"

"You'd be surprised to know who I am relying on these days."

"Boys," came a melodic but commanding voice, "this is a service of God. You will have to settle your differences away from here and at another time. It's all right, Mark, your father spoke with Pastor Marvin, and he gave his okay for Mr. O'Neil to be here." Mrs. Shultz was very womanly: healthy and curvy. Her dark hair hung in thick ringlets about her neck. She was struggling to tie it in a ribbon.

Cameron could see Mark struggling to swallow the snarl on his face as he took his seat. They were never friends. Mark Schultz had taken everything from Cameron: the partnership, which was rightfully his, at Brandon & Dobbs, and Shelly Madison, the one girl Cameron thought about changing his ways for. Shouldn't she be here? If she came, Cameron could use her to get in a few more digs at Mark. Cameron could see Mark scowling at him from his chair. Apparently, Christ didn't work everything out of a person right away. Cameron smirked to himself as he leaned his long frame against the wall in the corner of the room. He held his pen to his note-pad as if he was getting ready to record what he was seeing.

Mr. Schultz tried to creep in. Try was the operative term. The man was a blond version of Mark with graying temples. Only, if Mark was one football player, the elder Schultz was two. Shelly had told him over and over again about this man, Jacob Schultz. He had been a hard man, loathing anything and anybody unlike himself. The thought of people who were not white living in his neighborhood, let alone right next door to him was repugnant.

But when Shelly's little old grandmother Rose came, everything changed. She was everything right: smart and caring with the Wisdom of Solomon. The entire neighborhood thought so. And when Jake's own son fell in love with and married Shelly, well, Jake Schultz had two choices, "Get with the program or get left behind." Thinking about this made Cameron smile. Shelly did have a way with words. Jake, by his own admission, was not the smartest guy in the world, but he wasn't exactly a dullard either. Jake's surrender had brought an added benefit: his beloved Irene, a waif of a woman turned warrior under the tutelage of Mama Rose.

It was this same Irene Schultz who was preparing to conduct the meeting. Also in the circle was a little black woman with a hunched back and gnarled fingers. She rose slowly to her feet. A tall white man, who looked perfectly fit to Cameron, also stood. A small girl, of unknown origin with delicate features and super fuzzy hair, sat with her bowed head touching her knees. Those were the people worthy of note in Cameron's mind; the rest just blended in.

"Mr. O'Neil, you'll have to stand straight up for prayer and bow your head unless you'd rather kneel."

"I thought you understood, Mr. Schultz, I am here to observe only."

"Nobody observes only in my house when prayer is going on. So you have a few choices. You can bow your head and actually pray, you can bow your head and appear to pray, or you can pray for another healing service to observe while you make your way out the door. The choice is yours."

"Well when you put it that way." Cameron could see Mark's lips quivering. Oh, how he wished he could lay hold on the man and pound his fist into that insolent mouth, even the score once and for all. But focus was the order of the day. He needed answers, and for some reason he was convinced here was the place to find them.

He walked over to join the group as Jacob Schultz began, "Dear, Lord, thank you for gathering us in this place...we want nothing more than to be of service to you, for this is our reasonable sacrifice."

We ask nothing more and we give nothing less. The prayer of Cameron's childhood flooded his mind. He felt instant peace. **YOU DON'T HAVE THE NERVE TO PRAY. NOT YOU. LEAVE NOW AND NO ONE WILL KNOW YOUR REAL PURPOSE. I HATE YOU, GOD.**

"But I don't!" Cameron peeked from one eye to see if anyone had heard him. Was anyone looking his way? No one was. Concentrating on the prayer was not working anymore no matter how hard he tried. **GET OUT NOW. YOU KNOW WHOSE CHILD YOU REALLY ARE.** "Yes, I do," he surrendered. This whole venture was a farce. Maybe if he could ever be truthful, or real, something good could happen for him.

Tilting his head, he peered pitifully toward the door. Who was he trying to fool? If there was ever a devil's child... Quietly peering again over his shoulder, he noticed that the pathway to the exit was clear. He carefully pulled away from the hands holding his on either side and stumbled toward the door. Just as his hand touched the knob, a stronger hand planted itself on his shoulder. "Where do you think you're going, son?"

He turned to face Jacob Schultz. "Listen, sir, I never should have interrupted your service. My reasons for being here are clandestine like everything else in my life."

"Finally, truth," Mr. Schultz said wielding a smile that made Cameron feel calm. "You are on your way, young man; come on back in. Rejoin the circle, and leave your pad and pen in your pocket. Renie, my wife, is about to begin the healing prayer."

Cameron vaguely recalled getting back to the circle. A folding chair was quickly erected where he stood. Already there was a rising hum in the room, a crescendo of sound filling the space. He felt an airiness, a lightness. Its expression was physical, but not its source. He sat in that circle. Through a foggy haze he saw the muted blue of Mrs. Schultz's sleeve as she turned a small bottle to let a liquid drop onto her finger which she than dabbed on each person's head asking the Holy Spirit to tell her what they needed healing for. He remembered thinking how strange this was. Why couldn't each person simply tell her what his or her need was? When she rubbed the oily substance on his head, he found out.

"Lord Jesus, I feel in my heart that someone has come here today for a healing of the soul rather than of the body." His body quivered involuntarily, and he felt warm all over. *It's me,* he wanted to yell, but he couldn't or wouldn't. As Mrs. Schultz continued, he began to feel a sort of swell. It began in his belly and rose to his head. A salty wet taste registered on his tongue, and he felt a strong arm wrapped about his shoulders as if trying to hold him in place. For a long time he sat in a kind of haze wondering who was wailing so uncontrollably.

"It's alright, man, don't sweat it. God is just purging you of the stuff that's been weighing you down." He heard this, then he heard nothing. Then he heard sweet voices, like the ones angels must have. Finally, he had to know whose bitter sobbing was shaking his chair. He opened his eyes and noticed with blurry vision that the room was mostly cleared. He also noted that his palms were wringing wet. Saliva leaked from his mouth.

"Give the boy some room," a newly familiar voice belted. Cameron lurched toward a small lamp stand where he was able to grab a handful of tissue. Then to his absolute amazement and horror, Mark, the man who stole his life, was sitting right next to him. Mark was wrapped around him like a cheap sweater, holding him, engulfing him. He wanted to pull away. He felt disgusted. He was, in fact, disgusting. He jumped to his feet.

"I'm sorry... ladies and gen-tle-man," he could hear himself gulping for air. "This is not a good idea—"

"Cameron, there's nothing to be ashamed of." Mark was looking up at him with a sympathy so wide and deep, he would have cried for the person that look was meant for, had it not been for he, himself.

Schultz Sr. joined the chorus, "Young man, you never know if you will have another chance like this."

"Cameron, this is the acceptable day of the Lord. Salvation is near." He turned to look at the woman who had issued the invitational warning. He had to focus hard on her face. He had heard Mrs. Schulz speak before, but the commanding quality of her current speaking voice hardly seemed to emanate from her at all. He was breathing hard and fast. His shirt was wet and sticking to his chest, and his jacket was hanging off one shoulder. This was all too strange. He had to get out before he lost himself.

CHAPTER 10

Lingering

Mondays were the worst. They signified the end-less circle that had become his life. Cameron walked into the modest building owned by the Dobbs, Schultz & Brandon Advertising Agency which had been his second home for several years. The fact that Mark's name had been added to the marquee bothered him a little less today. But as he made his way to his inadequate office with its one narrow window facing the brick wall of Landiss Law he knew it was time, had been time for months. He pulled a legal sized tablet of stationary from his desk and began to write: *To Whom it May Concern*. Though he knew exactly whom it should concern, he didn't believe it truly concerned anyone there anymore. His pen was poised in midair.

How do you resign from a place that you thought was your own? Through their adjoining doors he called, "Marge, can you please come over here?"

Marge, still lovely and nearing fifty, had been one of the few women he had spared his attentions. He was never quite sure if she felt honored or neglected, probably a little of both. He shook his head thinking what a rake he'd been. He no longer felt pride in being such a shameless woman slayer. Anyway, after today that would hardly matter. He was going to take Anita's challenge. Whatever he was going to do, he wouldn't be doing it here.

Marge rolled her chair over, her cat-like glasses teetering on the bridge of her nose. "Yes, Cam, how can I help you?"

"Have I ever told you how lovely you are?"

"Yes, Cameron, many times."

"Both inside and out?"

"No, you have never put it that way. You, all right? You haven't been yourself lately. Can I tell you a little secret?" She pulled on his collar so his ear was near her peach colored lips. "If I wasn't worried about you, I'd be happy for you. Now how can I help you?"

Cameron leaned back in his rolling chair and adjusted the knot of his tie. As if pondering her words, he stood and walked to raise the one window that graced his office. He breathed in the Spring air and peered out at that awful brick wall view. Marge turned the notepad, on his desk, so she could see what he was starting to write.

"Good morning, Marge, Cameron," a booming voice interrupted.

"Mr. Schultz." Startled by the new arrival, Marge adjusted her blouse and sat up straight with her pen and pad at the ready.

"Marge, can you excuse me and Mr. O'Neil for a few minutes?"

"What do you want, Mark? Come to lecture me on my tardiness?"

"Cameron, I've come to offer you a job."

"I have a job, or am I being summarily dismissed by you?"

"Ahem," Marge grunted, scrambling to her feet and walking quietly past her towering employers.

"Cameron." Mark heaved a deep sigh. "I was going to drive out to Wisconsin to check out a business idea and property that our new client wants our agency to represent. He says I can spend a few days there if I want to."

"And you want me to go instead. I've been reduced to your errand boy. Is that it? What, can't you stand to be away from Shelly that long?"

"Cameron, I want to go, and believe me I could make a way for Shelly to come with me...but..."

"But what... What is this then, pity?"

"Cameron, you sure don't make it easy... If it wasn't for Him."

"Who? Kincaid working his wiles on the big bosses, trying to get me to back off his little girl?'

"No, Him!" Mark gritted, barely able to remain civil. "I'm not supposed to go. He wants you to go."

Cameron wanted to laugh, but Schultz was serious. "You mean Him, the big guy in the sky, Him?"

"You're mocking."

"No, I'm not. How does He speak to you?"

"At this point, He's roaring like a lion, and sometimes—"

"And sometimes He's like Hansel and Gretel leaving bread crumbs for you to follow."

"Couldn't have said it better myself."

"You need to go, Cam," Marge interrupted. "It might keep you from doing something rash." She approached gingerly. "Give you time to think," she finished, standing by her champion.

He knew she was right, but it was so hard to accept charity from Mark Schultz, but what if —

"Well, what's it going to be, Cameron?"

"I'll, I'll do it, Mark." Before he could think it through, he had extended his hand to Mark Schultz.

As he stood there, still staring at the palm that had voluntarily shook Schultz's, the man turned to speak.

"Hey, Cameron, do you realize that this is the first time we've had a conversation in which we referred to each other by our first names more than once?"

Indeed he had noticed. Maybe this solitary trip to Wisconsin would give him the opportunity to figure out why.

"Welcome back, Mr. O'Neil. How was your vacation?" Diane questioned from her desk in the middle of the brightly lit secretarial pool.

"And what's her name?" Amanda Cole —the lone woman ad executive of Dobbs, Schultz & Brandon—intoned.

She flipped his tie as she slithered by, her extra-long legs and extra-short red skirt causing even the women to turn and look. Amanda was the woman other women wanted to be but were afraid to be. She butted heads so often with men, they looked twice to make sure she wasn't perpetrating a hoax. Together, he and Amanda had hatched many a plot at Brandon & Dobbs. And they had fought many battles against each other for dominance and for Eric Brandon's approval, thinking that would get one of them the partnership. These days Cameron just couldn't force himself to desire or loathe her, to compete with her, or leave her to her own devises. Still her question lingered in his mind, "And what's her name?"

Cameron wasn't sure about a lot of things, but he knew for sure he was done with that. There was only one woman he wanted. He was also sure he couldn't continue to live as he had. He wanted to be out of this fish bowl so he could view it from the outside. He reasoned that as long as he swam with the piranhas he'd never be able to see himself as anything other than one of them.

It was decided then, change was the order of the day. *I'm going to buy that cabin,* he thought, that *cottage* as the "non-locals" called it. He liked "cottage" better. It conjured up images of Shangri-la: peaks and valleys with streams and brooks that ran over the earth's crust, penetrating both the land and the soul. Yeah, that was the first thing he was going to do. The next was to commit to Mt. Prospect and the third was to see what there was, if anything, with Anita Kincaid. Chuck Kincaid no longer frightened him. Nothing did.

Yes, thought Cameron, *sometimes He roars like a lion and sometimes, like Hansel and Gretel, He just walks ahead, dropping breadcrumbs, waiting for you to gather them and figure it out.*

CHAPTER 11

Surprise!

"I thought you lost interest in me."

Cameron had walked miles, thinking about this meeting, not bothering to go home after work. He certainly expected any salutation other than the one he received as the whoosh of wind accompanied him into Akiko Designs. He felt he ought to go out and come in again, and he would have, if her smile had not gleamed "possibility." "Where have you been, Cameron?" she continued as he stood before her adjusting his tie for no particular reason.

"Well, Anita," he said hanging his pinstripe jacket over the counter and feeling more sure of himself, "I've been contemplating my life and if you must know, thinking very seriously about you. And thanks for calling me Cameron without me having to prompt you. It makes me feel less a fool for what I am about to do."

"Are you going to rob me?" She twirled with her hands held high. "I am alone you see."

Cameron's eyes followed hers to the clock. It was 8:00, an hour past closing.

"Only if you count your heart. I have to have it." Cameron said taking her hand and gently leading her to the leather chaise where he'd seen lovers sitting contemplating jewelry meant to symbolize their future. He chose that seat hoping Anita would immediately understand. She followed sweetly.

"Cameron," her lips parted slightly and her eyes moistened. "What do you want with me? I am a neglected, rejected woman. No one respects my wishes or values my opinions. I am even less use to you than I was to... never mind. Mr. O'Neil—"

"Don't..," Cameron said sitting next to her.

"I don't understand."

"I know that you do. Don't shut me out." He grabbed her hands in his and peered into her eyes. "I'm telling you that I want you, that I love you. Anita, you are the only woman who makes me laugh. I know it sounds strange, but until I met you, I didn't realize that I rarely laugh."

"You are laughing at me?" She pulled slightly away.

"No, never, it's just that you get me. And I feel at ease with you. I want to tell you about the real me. About the things that caused me to be.... to be... the way I am. Have you ever thought about us? What I do to you?" He laid his hand near her heart. "Do you think you could love me too?"

"If I thought you really wanted me... no, I couldn't—"

"I want to marry you, Anita."

"Sure you do... " Sarcasm dripped from her words.

"Don't mock me, Anita. If you don't want me, say so. It'll probably kill me to do it, but I'll walk away and leave you alone. You may not believe me, but I've... well, I think I've changed. It's so new I can't be certain. But one thing has remained and that's the way I feel about you..."

"The way you feel about me, Cameron..." She became soft and leaned into his chest. She squeezed his hand and held it, looking down. He picked up her chin and stared again into her smoky black eyes.

"You care about me?" Anita questioned again.

"Yes, I've told you I do."

"But you have said words like this before, to other women? Many?" She was averting her eyes again.

"Not to you and not that I've meant until this moment," he pleaded.

He placed his hand on hers. She pulled away. He thought she was angry. She looked up at the squares of the sculpted metal ceiling.

"O'Neil, Yamaguchi... what difference, really."

"What?" Cameron asked pulling her chin to his line of sight. "What are you thinking, Anita?"

"I'm thinking. I would like to marry you. Yes. Let's do it. I will marry you, Cameron. We should do it right away and show the world."

As they stood in the middle of the floor with darkness coming down like curtains outside the glass windows and door, Cameron pushed past the churning at the edge of his mind. He chose rather to focus on the sensation of being just on the brink of complete happiness.

"Anita, I knew I couldn't be wrong about you. You won't be sorry. I will do whatever it takes to make you happy. I will be the man you want, and you will be my wife."

Cameron took her hand in his and pulled her to her feet. He cupped her face in his hands and looked into the eyes of the woman who had promised to make him the happiest man alive. There was the tiniest tear escaping from her shadowed lids. Then she perked up and smiled.

"It'll be okay," she whispered.

She was uncertain. At twenty-three, she was mature and poised but still young. He was a worldly man of thirty-one, and even he was nervous. This was a big step, who wouldn't be scared? They were going to be married, after all. He lifted his little bride-to-be above his head. Her black and yellow-print skirt flowed in her wake. She breathed in deeply, closing her eyes. When she opened them the tears were flowing full on. She cupped his face in her hands and met his gaze. "I do care for you, Cameron, I do." This was just the beginning. He was sure in time she'd be as happy as he was.

The road to marital bliss was taking a few strange turns. To start with, Anita would not allow him to take her home and inform her father of their plans. After the proposal, she said she would get home as usual and that he should go to his home and get some rest. "If you still want me, pick me up at 10:00 a.m. tomorrow. We will go and get the license together. Then as soon as the required time passes, we will get the deed done."

"The deed done, Anita. That sounds cold and calculating." He touched the tip of her nose, teasingly. "Anita," he cajoled, "your father is the master of formality and as enamored as he is with Japanese culture, I know he'll expect me to ask for your hand formally."

"My hand, Cameron." Her eyes narrowed. "My hand is mine to give. And do you actually think he'd give it to you?"

"No, actually I don't." He placed her coat delicately on her shoulders. "But I'd be doing this for you. I want to respect your father and his customs as much as I can. And there's no need to antagonize the man unnecessarily."

"So there it is."

"There what is?" he said, walking her to the door.

"Everyone's afraid of him. The world spins and flips on his say so."

"I didn't say all that. Still, he is a powerful man."

"I'm done with his power. Will you marry me or not?" she demanded, snatching her purse from the hidden drawer beneath the showcases.

"I will."

Her head dropped, as the floor seemed to claim her interest. "See you tomorrow, Cameron."

Diary: March 1, 1970

Anita is my wife. We got married today, the first day our license made it legal to do so. I wanted to at least let her family know about the wedding since she insisted we not tell them about our engagement. I didn't like keeping it from them, but in the end it was her decision and I didn't want to make a big deal of it. We were married before the Justice of the Peace. It wasn't romantic. I would not have chosen this, but then if Anita thought it was ok, I didn't think it should matter to me. "I love you Anita," I whispered it against her ear. She didn't respond. She wasn't ready. *It's okay. I can wait.*

CHAPTER 12

Home Sweet Home

The fortress loomed heavily above them just as it did on the night of Chuck Kincaid's trial-by-fire of the Brandon & Dobbs' top brass. It had been an uncomfortable night. He, Mark and Amanda knew that meeting the great man at his home meant they were all on trial: their manners, their work and their ability to handle pressure. That was over a year ago and Shelly, of all people, had helped Mark come up with the winning slogan and the key to promised partnership. Who would have imagined that she had studied Kincaid's product line? It also didn't hurt that Mark had dared buck society by marrying outside his race, as they all discovered that night, Kincaid had also done.

That had been a difficult night for Cameron. He didn't think this one would be so bad. He and Anita had been married one week. Right after the cere-mony, Anita had come to live with him. He wasn't sure what excuse she had given her parents, but he felt they had waited long enough to know that their daughter was married. Tonight was the night. Anita agreed. They pulled up to the gatehouse, and Cameron leaned out to announce their arrival.

"Mr. and Mrs.—"

Anita placed her hand over his mouth, "Just say Miss Kincaid for now, Cameron."

He wasn't sure what game she was playing, but it was her move. "Miss. Kincaid and guest to see Mr. and Mrs. Chuck Kincaid."

The attendant nodded from his high stool in his brush-shrouded gingerbread house and waved them on. They climbed the driveway to the ice castle. A servant rushed down the mountain of stairs, greeted them at the head of the circle and opened the door for them both. Cameron and Anita marched up the stairs, each a large platform, leading up to enormous white doors. There they stood. She squeezed his hand so hard it hurt. "Cameron, do we have to go in?"

He met her gaze. The anguish on her face was unmistakable. "What do you mean?" he asked. "You wanted to come, remember?" She was shaking her head, her pretty black hair moving from side to side. "Anita, we agreed to tell your parents right after we married. It's time they knew, approval or not."

She crowded in next to him, shaking like it was below zero, rather than a mere 40 something in

March. Instinctively, he gathered her in. A mortal dread came over him, "If you really don't want..." Before he could complete his sentence the great doors eased open and a white suited servant beckoned their entrance.

Anita squared her shoulders, straightened her face, released his hand, and said simply, "Let's get this over with."

Again Cameron recalled the first time he had been in the Kincaid home. From his mighty perch, the austere Kincaid had scrutinized him and each one of his colleagues. The memory of Kincaid assessing and re-assessing their capabilities and worthiness of representing his jewelry stores was still fresh. Due to Kincaid's influence both here and abroad, every Chicago advertising agency had been chomping at the bit to have him as a client. The irony of Cameron being here again to be appraised by the man was not lost on him.

This is a new day, Cameron thought, *and I'm hardly the same man Chuck Kincaid encountered all those months ago. This is for my wife, and I am up to the challenge.*

The walk down the hall to the meeting room was torturous and never-ending. Still the task before him would be but a mere formality if Anita wasn't behaving so strangely, first like a terrified child and then like…like…an ice princess. Suddenly everything inside him trembled.

Several more steps and finally they had arrived. The sight of Kincaid standing erect, wearing—as usual—a dark Kimono-like dress for men and a haughty smirk was actually a relief. His stance bespoke his usual arrogance, but his face was saying something else. Sadness…no…pity? But that didn't make any sense. Akiko, his demure little wife, stood evenly by his side wearing a light green version of his outfit and a definite expression of sympathy. The white-clad servant who had escorted them down the long broad hall bowed a hasty retreat and left the two couples staring at each other. Anita was so quiet he thought for a minute that he was there alone.

"Mr. Kincaid." Cameron marched up to him extending his hand to his…his father-in-law and was surprised when Chuck Kincaid matched his gesture.

"O'Neil." He nodded.

For a moment they said nothing. The opulent meeting room of emerald greens and layered plums and purples was accented with brass. The seating was low, almost as if one was expected to sit crossed legged on the floor. He was glad that their short meeting was conducted standing up.

"Mr. O'Neil, I'll get right to the point." Kincaid sneered releasing his grip. "Even you don't deserve what my daughter has done to you."

"Sir," Cameron said, tugging at the knot of his tie, "I had no idea what to expect on this occasion, but I certainly didn't expect this level of pettiness."

"You will have to address your bride with regard to pettiness." Kincaid's pointed features were drawn tight as he walked toward where Anita was standing. The long ornate room closed in on them as Anita groped the mantle for support. "Yes, Anita, I know about this farce of a marriage." He turned back to Cameron, who had to fight not to rush and strike him. "O'Neil, I regret to inform you that Anita's marriage to you is nothing more than an attempt to defy her mother and me. We told Anita's would-be fiancé that we did not approve of their engagement. Her intended, Harold, one of my employees…"

"You make him sound like a slave," Anita squealed, pale and stringy.

Her father continued, "Mr. Yamaguchi," he said, like it was a swear word, "did not fight me. He gave in immediately when I informed him that I didn't approve, that he'd lose his job and that Anita would be cut off financially if they married. Harold knew his limitations. And you, Mr. O'Neil," he pointed his long finger, "would do well to know yours. The same goes for you." He spun again toward Anita who had drawn back against the wall, her palms firmly planted against it. "She gets nothing from this marriage. You can cut your losses..." He kept talking, not bothering to turn around. "Our lawyer has prepared the paperwork for the annulment. I presume you haven't consummated it."

"It." Cameron dropped back. A sucker punch. The velvet green scarf hanging from the ceiling felt like a noose caressing his shoulder. He was literally seeing red. When he gained his breath, he noticed that the veins in his hands were hot and visible. Could Anita really be so scheming? He had been King Conniver. Could he have been this naive? Had his desire and male ego totally blinded him? Just because he had started trusting God didn't mean God trusted him. Maybe God thought he wasn't good enough to have real love in his life.

"I know that you have long been pursuing running your own ad agency," Kincaid spouted, glaring directly at him.

There it was again: that high-minded judge and jury baritone. Didn't this man have any idea how close he was to death?

"I personally don't think you are ready," Kincaid continued, "but—"

"Listen, Mr. Kincaid, I love Anita."

"Cameron, you don't have to do this..." Anita intoned, forcing herself to come near him.

Do this. She wasn't going to say it. Even he didn't deserve this. Hadn't he done everything he knew how to, to turn his life around and to prove his love to her?

"Cameron." She placed her delicate hand on his shoulder. It scalded like hot oil. "I'm sorry."

He turned to see her face, to really see it. That pained expression that he had seen a hint of the night he proposed to her was grotesquely exaggerated. Her face had become ugly to him.

"About the annulment," Kincaid sliced in.

"That's impossible." Cameron strode hard toward Kincaid.

"Mr. O'Neil," Kincaid continued a little less forceful, "I am prepared to make you a very rich man."

"You insult me, father." Anita moved to her father's side. "Cameron, I'm so sorry, but my father has correctly described my motivation, and I am ashamed to have done this... even to you."

Even me. "Anita, you don't know me at all, do you?" He searched her face for any hint of his Anita. "Have you not seen the difference in me?" *Was he actually begging her to accept him?*

"Cameron, I know what a good actor you can be." She gripped the golden mantle and spoke into space.

"You will not really be hurt to be rid of a woman who does not love you and who you do not really love."

"Yes, of course, a man like me is incapable of love and equally incapable of change. That's what you think." He jumped toward her. "That's really what you think? What you need to believe?"

"It is what it is," she rushed, stepping toward her father.

Cameron turned and walked toward the door, completely ready to live down to the expectations passed down from his own father and being indelicately expressed by Anita's father, when he remembered his ace in the hole.

"Mr. Kincaid." Cameron turned, hating the very sight of this warmly decorated room inhabited by cold fish. "I would be happy to start my own company with your money." He strode toward Chuck Kincaid. "That is if the new Mrs. O'Neil is not carrying my child," he growled, nose-to-nose with Kincaid.

"Mr. O'Neil." Kincaid backed up, ran his hands unevenly down his gown and chortled with a little less bluster, "A man of your vast experience must know that Immaculate Conception has only happened once and even that is up for debate."

"I beg to differ," Cameron spat.

Kincaid took another discrete step back. "You beg to differ with what?"

Kincaid's smugness was certainly not up for debate. That was until his head snapped toward Anita. Her deep coloring oozed from her face. She collapsed onto one of the low sofa-like seats.

"Anita…you didn't!"

"Anita —she did." Cameron squared his shoulders and walked over to the claw footed green velvet seat where Anita had squirmed. "And if you don't mind, my wife and my potential offspring will be leaving presently—with me."

Cameron grabbed Anita's sweaty wet hand and pulled his wife back down the never-ending hall. On the way in, the gold strands that threaded their way up and down from the seemingly mile-high ceiling had been heralds—heralds, he couldn't have chosen a different word? How about signs? —the gold strands had been signs arching toward heaven and pointing to the limitlessness of their possibilities. At this moment their direction seemed completely opposite, instead of extending up toward heaven, they signaled the direction he had been headed all his life. When he reached the gigantic doors that guarded this fortress, he was amazed to see that Anita still accompanied him.

He had to ask. "Why are you here?"

"I...I am defiled."

He wanted to push her back into the mansion, hard. Instead, he hauled her down the stairs so forcefully he couldn't recall if he had lifted or dragged her. Fortunately the car had been pulled up. He put a firm hand on her waist and to his dismay, shoved her in. He was ashamed. Of all his rakish behavior, he had never physically assaulted a woman. Though he was tempted today. He really was.

He hated her, but he wanted her, and he wasn't about to be denied; not this time. He had done everything right, and for once in his life things were going to turn out right for him.

CHAPTER 13

Two Ships

"Is he ever going to touch me again?" Anita tossed the tear-stained TV Guide on the table and laid her head on one of the three dingy pillows on Cameron's stiff narrow sofa. She had lived there over a month since that fateful night at her father's house. Outside the April showers were causing things to thaw; inside it seemed things were frosting over. For the first couple of days after their return, he had nothing to say to her, nor she to him. They slept in the same bed, he perfectly rigid on his side and she perfectly miserable on her side.

These days they were like prisoners sharing the same cell. If only they had not made love. What if they had never gone to her parents? Did she miss him?

It had been a chilly day and she wanted to make him something warm, she didn't. Her head snapped up toward the jangling of keys at the door. It was him. "Good evening, Anita," he said, in the same formal manner he had used since their return.

"Hello, Cameron, would you like some tea?"

He turned slowly toward her like he was trying to see who she was today. "Yes, I would."

Sitting at their tiny dining table he waited. She poured the liquid from the kettle on the stove and silently scolded herself for not taking the time to turn the knob on the burner to let the flames warm the pot. He drank it anyway, eyeing her suspiciously.

"Anita," he continued, one arm on the table the other supporting his tepid cup of tea, "I've been thinking."

"Yes."

"We are married. Shouldn't we..."

"If you wish," she cut in not looking up from the heavy miss-matched coffee cup she had taken from Cameron's disorganized cabinet.

"If I wish?" He looked up. "Yes, Anita, I wish," he spat getting abruptly to his feet and making his way to his crowded bookcase. "I wish..." he ran his hands over his hair, "never mind. We will sleep together tonight. Is that alright with you?" His elbow was posted against his shelf and his hand covered his mouth. He blew an exasperated breath like he was trying to get through to an idiot. For the life of her she couldn't figure out why she just didn't give in.

That night she was giddy with excitement on the in-side. Cameron didn't need to see it. As she did most nights she sat on the couch waiting for him to make the meager meal. He made baked ham and green beans. She could only eat a little. He took a book off his shelf and grabbed the Sun-Times and Tribune.

"Are you going to read all those?"

"Yes, dear," he said sarcastically sitting on the end of the couch.

"Why do you read so much?"

He smiled. "This is how I received my formal ed-ucation. You see I never really went—"

"Never mind," she cut in. The green light in Cameron's eyes went dim. He looked rather like a wet cat, not at all pleased. She had no idea why. At 9:30 he went into the bathroom. Anita used the time to quickly undress and kick pressed shirts, t-shirts, socks, pants—that needed to go to the cleaners—and assorted papers off the foot of the bed. Cameron was not really a slob. Everything had a place, sort of, but not much was in its right place. He needed a housekeeper.

For almost an hour she checked and double-checked the gold-plated clock on the night-table. Did he always take this long to prepare for bed? She waited with her hands firmly gripping the sheet she held snuggly under her neck. When she saw the light under the bathroom door go out, she dimmed the light in the bedroom.

He opened the door and stood bare-chested staring at her. Even in the low light she could see that there was wanting in his eyes, which went beyond the natural. He wanted something more from her then this bed had to offer. She stared. There was no more. Nothing. She didn't have anything else. Maybe she should. Maybe she could if she cared for him in the way he seemed to care for her. Her mind reeled. She willed herself to stop this train of thought. He wanted her for the same reason she wanted him, revenge.

She closed her eyes against the longing she had seen in his eyes, but his scent was filling her. Her mind recalled how his dewy hair fell over his brow. Her arms involuntarily reached for him. He came to her. They wound themselves into one, and for a brief moment, there was no separation, none.

Days turned into weeks. Anita thought about how well her marriage was starting to work. Each morning she'd sleep in, savoring the impassioned nights she and Cameron had shared. Most days Cameron would be gone by the time she got up, usually around 10:00 a.m. Sometimes she'd go in. "Anita, do you still work here?" Shelly would quip.

After several days of missed work Anita thought she'd better make an appearance. To her surprise a fresh-faced blonde was there.

"Hello, Ma'am, welcome to Akiko Designs where only the finest can be found. How may I serve you?"

"Where is Shelly Schultz?" Anita paced glaring at the girl. "Get her out here!."

"Mrs. Schultz is taking the day off, Ma'am. But I bet you are wondering who I am." Without giving Anita time to respond, she launched into her story, "I came in two weeks ago to find the store packed with women. One lady, a Mrs. Greer, bought a beautiful jade bracelet for her daughter. They talked over there by the bonsai trees and that cute little oriental fountain. I love the decor here. You must love it too." Anita was too stunned to answer. "Anyway those women, 'pete and re-pete,' whispered and pointed for at least thirty minutes about which Akiko creation they most admired. A Miss Cacaran," she searched the sky for an answer, "yes I believe that was her name, she purchased that one-of-a-kind carnelian ring. Poor Mrs. Schultz was ice-skating across the floor trying to accommodate one, then the other. I wasn't busy so I volunteered to help her out. Sounds strange, doesn't it? But I wasn't here to buy anything. I was just admiring the rings. Anyway, when I was done…" She smiled brilliantly flipping her light blond hair over her black collared dress, "Mrs. Schultz asked me if I wanted the job permanently. I did, so here I am." Her up-turned palms and splayed fingers punctuated this announcement.

"Yes, here you are." Anita looked at her mother's empty shop and wondered were all these people were who couldn't stand to wait an extra minute or two to be taken care of.

"Oh, my goodness, look at the time." The freckled-face youth chirped looking bug-eyed at her watch, "I'll be taking a short break in a few minutes."

"Are you closing the store then, until you return?" Anita arched one eye while squinting out of the other.

"Goodness no. Mr. O'Neil will be here to cover for me in fifteen minutes."

"Mr. O'Neil, my…er….does he come here often?"

"What a strange question from someone who should be here often herself."

"Cameron!" Anita whirled toward his clipped voice.

"Yes, dear, Miss Radcliffe was just telling me how the woman who used to work here simply stopped showing up. What have you been doing with your days?"

Anita felt shocked and off guard. What was going on here? "Me...I...I have been. I...well I. It's none of your business what I have been doing." She hardened. "Who are you to question me? And you..." Anita turned, marching toward the interloper—who instantly became a simpering vine, not the strong tree she had been just three minutes ago. Miss Radcliffe, hands trembling and sniveling, shrank out the door leaving them to each other. Fortunately it was a slow afternoon.

"I have a question of my own," Anita sniped at her husband. "What, tell me, are you doing here covering for Miss, Miss Radcliffe?"

"A n i t a," he drawled heavily, "as your husband I would have been happy to tell you what I was doing here with Kimberly. But as your cast-off, I am under no obligation to divulge information of any kind to you."

"So, you will not tell?" Her voice was quavering and unattractive.

"So, I will not tell," he said flatly rolling up his sleeves with his back turned to her. "And you are no longer needed here," he barked. "You," he paused for emphasis, "may leave."

You may leave. It was not a request but a command, and the words still stung. After gaping at Cameron's back for several long seconds, she turned to clutch the over-sized door handle. She didn't dare stay. It felt too much for her. Her ankles felt wobbly, and it made her want to throw up thinking about Kimberly and Cameron wiping down counters and putting away hidden treasure. She stood outside shivering in the harsh wind with the sun darting in and out of rippled clouds for several minutes before she realized that Cameron would not be coming after her. Slowly she made her way home.

Clutching the arms of the big chair, Anita sat staring out of their bedroom window. She had watched television until the TV snow can on, so there were no more programs to distract her. And outside it was dark, very dark. The Deli lights were turned off and no one was walking the street. Cameroon, she moaned in the back of her throat. It didn't matter why they were together, they were. She didn't want to lose whatever part of him she had. It seemed he was becoming untouchable to her. Even his body didn't seen to want her in the way it once did. Cameroon, she moaned again, feeling moisture press against her eyes. Then she heard the squeaking of the boards outside their door. Quickly she jumped from the claw foot chair and ran to their bed. Cover up, she told herself, pulling up the mound of blankets, there's no need for him to know I waited up.

It was Wednesday, and after covering, yet again, for Kimberly Radcliffe—helping a young bride-to-be pick a wedding band she could afford and her fiancé would love–it occurred to Cameron that he really did want to please his wife. They could begin again. He'd take her on a trip. Anita had once talked about making the Manzanar Pilgrimage to see the place where her Japanese grandfather had been interned after WWII at Camp Amache. It wasn't romantic, but he thought she'd like to know that he paid attention to what mattered to her, and they could go to the ocean. Maybe she'd like to see it again. He still had time to stop at the library on the way to church. He knew just where the books on Japanese American history were kept.

While Cameron sat in Pastor Marvin's office, surrounded by file cabinets filled to the brim with baptismal certificates for just about every member of Mt. Prospect along with donation envelopes and offering pans, finishing his research on childrens'

camps for the youth department and starting to look over the books he'd gotten from the library, Brother Ramos, sweating and breathing hard, peeked in.

"Brother Cameron, do you have time to help me get this stuff moved out of Pastor's office? It has to be done tonight so that the painter can get to the walls in the morning, and I want to get home soon." Cameron leaped to his feet, glad for an excuse to move around and do something that didn't involve sitting. He stumbled at the door, nearly knocking over three small children standing in his way. "Can we help?" the eldest, a girl, yelped, her dark ponytail bouncing as she jumped. Ramos shook his head vigorously.

"Why don't you all draw us some pictures," Cameron compromised, retrieving notebook paper and pencils from the pastor's desk for the children.

He and Ramos were just about done jostling heavy boxes up and down the narrow hallway when the phone in Pastor Marvin's cramped office rang. Ramos ran in to pick it up, leaving his children quietly drawing superheroes and mermaids in the corner. He rushed out panting and pleading, "Please, Brother Cameron, can you watch my children? My Miranda is very sick, and I need to take her to the hospital. Here take the house keys." He twisted two from his ring. "Theresa knows how to get home. You can walk there. Please watch her and her brothers until I return." Cameron was about to speak when Ramos continued, "Thank you, brother, I can hardly believe what a bad man you used to be."

Cameron again opened his mouth to utter a number of things, one being, "How did you know I was a bad man?" when he looked down at chubby-cheeked Theresa as she smiled up at him. Hissing through her missing front tooth she spoke, "Come on, Poppa say. Come on, let's go home." She pulled on his pant leg as her brothers began to tear up. Mr. Ramos was gone and his key was in Cameron's palm, so he bent down to dry Carlos' tears and give Antonio a stick of Wrigley's spearmint gum he'd had in his pocket for a week. They walked the block or so humming, "Yes, Jesus Loves Me."

When they arrived at the run-down building with no entry lights or locks on the ground level door, Cameron's heart sank. Ramos was a nice, hard-working man. He shouldn't have to live like this. Cameron's eyes were traveling up the rickety fire escape when Theresa yanked his pant leg again. "Come on, let's go." They went down the dark stairs at the side of the building to a basement apartment, which was right around the corner from the furnace. Cameron was pretty sure this dwelling was in violation of several codes. But when he unlocked the door to the Ramos', their sparsely finished place was immaculate.

Cameron removed their little coats and helped them put their pajamas on and asked Theresa to get him a book. Apparently they had only the Bible. A good book to be sure, but the kids could use some others. Note to self, Cameron thought, buy some books for Theresa, Carlos, and Antonio. He read from the Psalms, skipping the harsher parts. He laughed gently thinking he had never thought of Psalms as a dangerous book before. An hour passed, and it was only 9:00 p.m. so he sang made-up songs to the kids and asked them dumb riddles with no answers. They laughed and giggled their way to sleep. Immediately he got up from the floor next to their mattresses and looked for a phone. Just when his hand reached the dial of the green wall mount, he remembered her words, "Who are you to question me?" *Only your husband.* Nothing had really changed since that day at Akiko's. In her mind she'd owed him no explanations. It bothered him not to call, but he thought it best. She couldn't always be taking him for granted.

Cameron walked back to the church with thoughts of children occupying his mind. The Ramoses were gracious, loving kids.

He and Anita would get past this rough patch. He loved her, and he believed deep down she loved him. And when they the learned to live together, they'd have a few kids of their own and life would be better.

He didn't remember the drive home, not a good sign. He was tired. Trudging up the stairs to his tiny apartment, he thought, we'll have to move when we have children. This place was okay for him, and when he mentioned moving to Anita she'd said it didn't matter where they lived, so here they stayed. The location was great, so why push it? But when the children came they'd need more room. Wisconsin might be nice.

He wondered if Anita was awake. He was looking forward to sharing the events of the day with his wife. Yes, his wife. They could try again.

He clicked the wall switch; it took his eyes a minute to adjust. Dirty dishes were still on the sticky table. The clothes Anita had worn where thrown over the back of the couch right next to a hanger, and the stale smell of breakfast and lunch pans lingered in the air. He knew she had not worked much, if at all, over the last several weeks. He couldn't conceive how anyone could find so much to do in a place this small which precluded even a small amount of cleaning. He was no mean housekeeper himself, but this bordered on filth. Who in the world had he married?

His shoulders slumped. He couldn't do it. He just couldn't start straightening up tonight. Instead he lumbered toward their room. She was asleep. Hadn't cared enough to wait up for an explanation. He got into the bed roughly and covered up to his neck.

"Cameron," he heard against his ear, "where have you been?" She shook him gently. Her concern pleased him.

He perched his mouth to answer.

"Never mind. I know what men like you do." This did not please him. He punched his pillow, rolled over to his side of the bed, and for the first time admitted to himself what kind of woman he had married.

Anita climbed the creaking stairs huffing and blowing. Each step seemed higher than the last, and her arms pulled under the weight of the bags she carried. She had gone to Saks on Michigan Avenue to purchase the pretty blue dress she had seen on display for herself, then to Carson Pirie Scott for an orange one with gold paisley at the hem. Cameron seemed to favor bright colors. She might wear it. She really wouldn't need these new clothes if she had anything worthwhile to do. She had sniped at the salesgirl when she told her she could not get the size five dress zipped up. "What do you mean this is not my size?" Anita had yelled. "My father is a very important man. If he hears how you are treating me…"

"I am so sorry, Ma'am, perhaps a different designer or brand?"

"Never mind. Just give me the seven!" *Incompetent woman. What am I thinking? It's not her fault. It's this sitting around all the time that's causing my waist to get bigger and bigger.*

With the memory of the shopping fiasco seared into her brain, Anita turned the key in the lock and plopped down in the chair nearest the door. Resting her head on the table, she allowed the little steam that had been rising in her chest to flow. Tears wet her cheeks. She was a failure. How had she gotten here? She used to travel, study her father's businesses, and attend school here and abroad.

Her father worshipped her. "What is your desire, my princess," he would say.

"I want the world," she would reply.

"Then I'll serve it to you on a platter." It was that way right up until she decided to stop attending school, almost two years ago. Then he started to ask her questions, "Why, Anita? You are so close to finishing. Your mother and I have great hopes for you. After all, one day you will run my empire."

They didn't know her plans, but she did. College dormitories filled with perky man-hunting co-eds bored her. Walking from class to class loaded down with heavy dull books was more than tiring. Those talk-talk-talk professors reminded her of her father's speeches. She wanted no more. What she did want was Haruto Yamaguchi. He was a very tall man for their people. He was dark and fun. Harold, as they called him here, was from the homeland. She had admired him from the time he was a teen until the present.

She still remembered their first kiss by the river. The dark waters flowed as she stood by him under the *momiji* tree. He had pushed her hair behind her ear and kissed her gently. He would take her away from the rule of her overbearing father and the silliness of her simpering mother. He was her refuge, intelligent and powerful. Surely the man in charge of her father's Tokyo interests was a good enough match for her. "If it pleases your father, I will ask for your hand," Haruto had said. She knew he was traditional, and she knew her father would say "yes."

It was only months ago that he had visited the U.S. and, as promised, he came to her home. She'd waited near her father's favorite meeting room, twiddling her thumbs, and shaking her leg from the haughty antique chair just outside his door. Harold had everything her father admired: skill, experience, success. Nothing her father could object to, she mumbled to herself. Besides, if she wanted him, her father would not say "no."

Harold didn't notice her at first as he rushed past her into the meeting. It was brief. Good news, of course. "Harold!" She had jumped to her feet.

"Anita, I'm afraid we will not be married," was all he said as he bowed and made a hasty retreat down the hall.

She ran into her father's lair to find him standing there in his princely robes. "I'm sorry, Anita."

"What did you do? What did you say to him?" She'd wept. Her father held out his arms for a hug. She embraced him then pushed away, "No! What did you say to him?" she repeated.

"He's not good enough for you, Nita," was all he said.

"He's not afraid of you."

"He is."

"He would not give me up for a job."

"He did."

"You are a liar."

"And you, my daughter, are hurt. It will pass, and you will see that I am right. Haruto is not good enough for you."

She peppered him with insults, accused him of not caring and of being unduly influenced by her mother, who of course was jealous of her. She didn't know what propelled her to say such nasty things, but once she started she could not stop.

The next day she was in her room, gaily trying on the black and yellow skirt that her mother had purchased for her in Europe, when she heard a knock on the door.

"Go away," she yelled.

"I cannot," Kim Kai pleaded. "Mr. Kincaid says to put on your new skirt. He has a surprise for you."

Anita primped in her head-to-toe gilded mirror and sprayed herself from her black perfume pump. She stroked her hair one hundred times then came out of her room. She knew her father couldn't stay mad at her. He never had before, but then she had never been so cruel and thoughtless before, at least she didn't think so.

Kim Kai walked her down the stairs, making sure she got her coat and continued to the driveway. Her father's favorite chauffeur, Harry, was in the car. "Is my father taking me to the new supper club with the jazz musicians? Do they have a lunch performance?"

Harry shook his head and said, "Get comfortable, Miss Anita."

She had watched the wind blow the trees, and even though it was cold, she rolled down the window to let the crisp chill wake her. They stopped at the jewelry store that her mom was supposed to work at and never did.

That day she found out that her punishment was to do more of her mother's job, not less. Her father explained that this lapse of judgment she was displaying, was precisely the reason he had her at the shop. She needed to slow down and get some perspective. More work, not less, was needed to focus her idle mind. She insisted again that Haruto loved her and would not stand to see her treated badly. He smirked. It wasn't happy or sad. He said, "If Haruto really wants you, I will honor your request."

*If he really wants you...*Those words still haunted her. Haruto didn't want her enough. Cameron had wanted her. Did he still? Everything was up-side-down, so confusing, so wrong.

CHAPTER 14

Calm Seas?

All of a sudden the storm was over. Their nights of passionate love had ended. Mild whispering calm was their life.

Cameron had stopped approaching her to make love, speak of love, or to act like he was in love. Passion seemed to be reserved for his God, whom he spoke and sang to quietly in their room. It was like she wasn't even there.

She sauntered out of her bedroom into the living room where Cameron was sitting.

"Reading, again?" she said sitting on the couch next to him, her thin slip sticking to her burgeoning curves. She sat very close to him, close enough to feel his breath as he mouthed the words to some clunky ad, "The glisten and glow to let your hair go, or should it say grow?" He scratched through the line with his pencil.

"Depends on who we're marketing it to I guess?"

"What?" he spared her a look.

"Well," she added, glad to have his attention, "for women with straight hair you could say glow and for women with thick bushy hair like Shelly, you can say grow. Afro-American women seem always interested in getting their hair to grow. And you know white women want their hair to shine, so…"

"That's good. Thanks." He nodded and smiled with just the corner of his mouth. Then he twisted past her to grab an eraser to make the changes.

"Cameron." She inched closer to him. "Can we, can we…"

Was he actually going to make her say it? A wife shouldn't have to ask, but she missed him so badly. She missed his touch and what they seemed to be able to share only when they were intimate. This was intolerable. Mother would know what to do. She'd call as soon as Cameron was asleep.

"Nita, it's you?" her mother whispered on the other end of the line.

Rocking with her knees pulled as close to her chest as she could get them and between sobs and sniffles, she was able to answer, "Yes, mother."

"Your father says you cannot call here so much. Three times a day, Nita. He very mad. You've done a bad thing this time," her voice halted.

"Mother?"

"Anita," her father's voice broke in, "you are a spoiled child, but what you have done this time is to make yourself a woman. I cannot protect you. I don't know what you are going to do…" his voice went quiet. She was worried. Even after all that had passed between them she knew they loved her. "Anita, I'm not sure, but I may have misjudged O'Neil. Anyway, I lo… Listen, don't call here for a while. Try being the adult you have so wanted to be."

She thought she heard a tear in her father's voice. He was a hard man. Tears were rare and regulated. If she had induced them, then her heart was truly going to break. No hugs from mother, no hugs from father. She was desperate for touch. She was desperate for Cameron's touch.

Another week went by. Cameron's annoyance with her was growing. He only spoke to her when necessary, and her parents forbade her to call home. Even

Shelly ignored her. She said as long as "nonsense" was the language, they had nothing to say to each other. Anita never imagined her so heartless.

She climbed into their overstuffed, cushiony wedding bed and pulled the covers around her shivering body. She was so lonely, so painfully lonely. Couldn't Cameron see her suffering? She had not gone out of the apartment in two days and she was coming down with a virus. If she got sick to death that would serve him right, treating her so dreadfully.

Anita awoke to wet covers and a pool of drool. How many hours had it been? She rolled over to check the clock. She peered through her aching eyes: 5:50. 5:50? She missed Cameron more than when she had laid down at 10 that morning.

Mother would help. Mother knew about "man things." Anita rolled weakly to her side and squinted against the faint light to dial her parents' number.

"Mother," she whispered as if she might be overheard.

"It's okay, Nita, your father is not here. Are you okay?"

"No, mother. My…er…Cameron, mother, he will not touch me." She sniffed, pulling heaps of tissue from her Kleenex box to blow her nose

"You want him to? If you get with a baby your father will not let you return."

"I know, mother, but I'm so lonely. I actually feel sick."

"You sick, Nita. Chuck will let you come—-"

"Not sick, mother. I'm miserable."

"What can I do, Nita? Your father has forbid—"

"Tell me the secret." Anita peeked around her crowded bedroom as if looking for spies.

"You mean—

"Yes, mother. You said you'd tell me the *forbidden touch* when I was married. Well I'm married," she squealed and blew her nose hard.

"And what of Harold?"

"Who?"

"Oh...but Nita, this for 'real-marriage.'"

"Mother, I want my husband to love me."

"You mean to be intimate with you. This will not bring love to a loveless—"

"Mother, just tell me!"

Anita felt dreadful and not just because Cameron was so evil to her. Well that wasn't exactly true; he had been fairly attentive and even kind the last few days even though she was so sad she barely moved. He quietly came home from work and ate whatever she cooked. She didn't put a lot of effort into the meals, but she had begun to feel guilty doing nothing. Today she felt too tired to make even her regular fare. He'd be home in an hour, then she'd get up.

Anita awoke an hour and a half later, sick because she hadn't eaten or cooked. Cameron was rattling his key in the door. "Come here, Anita," he called. There was almost tenderness in his voice; she was delirious. She carefully raked her tired legs over the mound of covers she had kicked up. "Coming," she managed between gritted teeth.

She dragged her body over to one of Cameron's long-legged dining chairs. Her bare feet lightly touched the floor. When she could get her eyes totally opened, she felt her mouth turn up. Cameron had brought home a delectable looking meal, and she was so hungry. She propped her elbows up on the table to support her heavy head.

"Come here, Anita."

"I can't, Cameroon."

"Sure you can, and did you call me Cameroon?"

"Yes, I've called you that when I'm alone. It sounds cute." *My god, what am I thinking to say such a thing?* "Cameron, I didn't mean…"

"Please don't take it back."

He seemed pleased. She wanted to please him again, so she willed herself to obey his directive. She walked over to him. To her surprise, he pulled her into his lap and wrapped his strong arms around her. She didn't know why, but she wanted to cry.

"Cameron, please, love me again." She looked at his face. He grimaced. He hated the idea of loving her. She remembered being spoiled, as her father called her, getting everything she wanted; but what she wanted now her father couldn't get for her, not this time.

"Please, Cameron." She realized she was begging, and she didn't care.

"No," she heard him say. More tears, begging to come out, burned her eyes.

"But why, I want you to."

"You want me to what?" the warmth of his breath teased her hair.

She grabbed his face and rubbed her hands down his cheeks, over and over again, as she had seen her mother do to her father. She didn't know what affect she was having on him. He picked her up and was taking her to the bed. "No, Cameron." She was clutching at his neck. "Only if you come too."

"You want me to make love to you? I thought—"

"Yes, I want you to be with me again." He was carrying her to bed where she had been sleeping alone, and she just couldn't go there again, not by herself. She struggled against his tight grasp, and he simply made it tighter. He put one knee on the bed and tried to unroll her into that mound of covers that didn't do a thing for her. She wrapped her arms around his neck. "Please, Cameroon," she heard herself whisper against his cheek.

The next thing she felt was his hands firm against her sides. It didn't feel mild. It felt intense and then they were gone. She surprised herself by grabbing his wrists before he could completely pull away. She pulled him down onto her body. She looked into his ocean green eyes. The tide was turning, a mix of fire and ice. There was a war raging in this man, and she felt her power. It was the power her mother said a woman possessed. There was no going back. With just the right touch, she would have him. She was afraid, but he was her husband, and it was about time she was his wife. She squeezed her eyes shut and did what her mother told her to do. Nothing happened so she peeked out of one eye. He froze, looking at her like he had never seen her before. Suddenly his hands were back, touching, loving, taking her just where she wanted to go.

She had never known anything like this. There was power and tenderness at the same time. When their lovemaking was over, he tried to leave their bed. She wrapped him in her embrace and subdued him, again, with her woman's powers. She was proud of herself. Today she was an adult. Today she was a woman.

CHAPTER 15

Taken

Anita zipped into her apartment, tossing her beige handbag at the lamp table. Out of sheer boredom, she'd stopped by the jewelry store to see if Cameron was covering the lunch break. He wasn't. It was Wednesday, so she was surprised to see that he hadn't come home yet to gather "the good books." She plunked down on the couch and pushed at the large burgundy Bible on the table. His plain speaking black one set next to it. He kept the blue one with him at all times. *With him at all times.*

She stared up at the ceiling. Was she actually jealous of a book? Her hands trembled as she reached for "Big Burgundy" and froze before she actually touched it. She couldn't. This was nonsense. Who could believe in this absent God of theirs? So much crime and pain. If he had been alive all those years ago, he was surely dead now. She blew a steadying breath and put her feet up on the table. The Bible Concordance and Commentary were there on the edge. Who was this fanatic she had married and where was he, anyway?

Anita jumped to her feet and rushed into their crowded room. Rambling frantically over the small corner desk, she snatched and pulled notes, receipts, tablets, calendars and finally the Yellow Pages to the surface: Brandon & Dobbs, Brandon & Dobbs, she thumbed through the alphabet, got it. She plunged her finger into the rotary and dialed the number to her husband's place of business. Funny, her finger seemed fat in the dial.

Click. She heard the rustling of a notepad and the rumbling of women's voices. "Hello. Yes, hello. Mr. O'Neil please," Anita said while twisting the knob on the bedroom fan, causing the metal blades to rattle into action. It had to be the hottest July day this year.

"I'm sorry, Miss..."

"Mrs."

"Mrs., er... who?"

"Mrs. O'Neil." Anita rolled her eyes, flopping down onto the wad of blue sheets at the end of her unmade bed while kicking off her high-heeled shoes.

"Cameron's ...? Oh, I'm sorry. Mrs. O'Neil, your son no longer works here. He didn't leave a forwarding number."

"My son! It sounds like I'm old enough to have a son Cameron's age?" Anita bolted upright, yanking the red silk scarf from her neck.

"Then I don't understand."

"His wife. I'm his wife. He's talked about me, yes?"

"No. Who is this really?" the woman questioned, giggles tickling her voice. "Miss Cole, is this you? Somebody look in Amanda Cole's office. See if she's in there."

"Who is this?" Anita was yelling, holding the receiver like she was scolding it.

"Marge, front desk secretary, Mr. O'Neil's former secretary. Listen, if you really are Mrs. O'Neil," she said with a chortle, "then you must know that Mr. O'Neil has not worked here for months. I'm so sorry. Please excuse me if I was rude. I just couldn't believe Cameron had a wife and one he has never mentioned."

Anita hung the phone up so hard she was surprised that the cradle didn't split in two. What was this? Her lip trembled involuntarily. Cameron had been dressing more casually and had totally ceased complaining about his job. Was he even still working?

Steaming and ready to pounce, Anita marched into the living room when she heard the key jiggling in the lock. If he was lying to her about work, what else was he hiding from her?

Cameron pushed their flimsy apartment door open and walked carefully over the threshold. His blond hair was sweaty and not combed, and his new-plastic-smile was plastered in place. He had obviously had a hard day doing something. She moved to pull his perfectly sized jacket from his shoulders and carefully hung it in the hall closet. His eyes followed her with a kind of suspicion.

"What is wrong?" she quizzed.

"Nothing," he said just quickly enough to let her know that he was lying.

"So, Cameron, how was work today?

"Fine. Why do you ask? I can't remember the last time you asked me about work."

He sat down at their small dinette table. "Anita," he said with all the formality he reserved for people he shared no intimacy with. She knew because he had used it on her in the days immediately following their introduction as husband and wife to her father and mother.

"Anita, we've been together for almost five months," he continued.

"Yes, many months." She pounded her hand on the table, "You'd think you'd tell your wife you'd changed jobs, and those women at your office, you never told them about me, did you?"

He rubbed his fingers over his forehead. "You see, Anita, this is what I wanted to talk to you about. Do you think any of this was easy for me?" His voice took on steam. "I tried telling you about my job with the church."

"The church again? That place. It's always about that place."

"Anita, listen to me. I've been trying to tell you, it's about God. Him being my father."

"Your father," she laughed, walking away. "Why are you being weak, Cameron? I expect this from my mother but not you."

"Akiko is not weak. In fact she is anything but. You yourself said she'd never defy your father, and I'm pretty sure Chuck Kincaid is not on board with his wife following the Christian God."

"Yes, well." Anita could feel her logic cracking under the weight of Cameron's reasoning. "I don't understand her. And I don't understand you either." She folded her arms and turned her back.

"Anita." Cameron stood and walked over to where she was, placing his hands on her shoulders. "I tried telling you about leaving D.S.B. and you acted like you are acting now."

She whirled on him, shrugging away from his hold. "I won't be part of this. I'm not listening.

And why," she yelled, "Why didn't you tell those people at Dobbs, Schultz & Brandon about our marriage?"

Cameron walked away, hands flailing. "Why, why would I tell the people at D.S.B. about my farce-marriage to a woman who only married me to mock her parents? Remember when you used to say I should quit? But now, now, Anita, you couldn't care less about anything that matters to me. You married me to take revenge on your parents for not letting you marry the man you really wanted."

Yes at first, she thought to correct, but remained silent.

Looking directly but wearily into her eyes, he waited and then sighed. "Anita?"

She wanted to respond, she really did.

"Anita, this has become an untenable situation for both of us." Anita's mouth felt slippery-sour and her knees began to wobble. "Anita, I've come to a decision that will serve us both in the end. You will go home to your parents."

No, she heard in the back of her throat, but no words came out.

"I've met with an attorney. If you will just sign…"

Anita sat with a thud, holding on to the table, her head swimming.

"….. we will both be free to pursue what we really want in a marriage."

No, echoed again somewhere in her muddled thoughts.

Cameron dug into his brown leather satchel producing a huge stack of papers. He pushed the cursed, print-filled mountain at her.

Her mind searched desperately for an escape and landed on her tenth birthday.

It had been a glorious day, sunny, and bright. She, her mother, and father pranced and danced their way down Westmier Street, flitting from shop to shop. Daddy's bags loaded with new dresses, shoes, and hats, and mother complained that she could not hold one more Hot Wheels set or Barbie doll. That's when they spotted it. It jutted forward like a spring in the desert: Pet World.

"My parakeet!" she had shouted.

"Anita, if we go in, we get the parakeet and leave. Yes?"

"Yes, Mama." Anita broke into a run and was waiting, bent over, breathing hard, and holding her knees when her parents found her by the bird cages and displays.

"Well, Nita, we are here."

Anita stood up looking this way and that. Birds chirped loudly, filling her ears with clatter and drowning out her mother's singsong announcement. Feathers, green, blue, and yellow tickled her nose, making her sneeze. And the mess at the bottom of the flapping and yelping creatures' cages: seeds, poop, and something that looked like a mush of all of that made her stomach lurch.

"I want a puppy!" She grabbed her father's arm and pulled him recklessly through crowds of standing children oohing and aahing over several puppies sitting behind a glass wall.

"Nita, no," her mother cried. "We said bird. You will take care of a bird. No dog. I say, no."

"Daddy, please, I promise." She looked up at her tall, slender, handsome father. He dropped his bags and folded his arms across his chest shaking his head, no. Her mother smiled. Anita cried, tugged on the bottom of his suit coat. He looked down, brushed her bangs away, and looked at her mother pleadingly. Her mother shook her head, no. Daddy shook his head, yes. Twenty minutes and twenty dollars later, they walked hand-and-hand, all three, out of the pet shop door, her new puppy, Charms, wagging happily behind. Funny thing is, she took care of that dog right up until the day he died. She got what she wanted, and she took care of it.

Give me one more chance, Cameron, she pleaded in her heart, but her lips did not move.

She blinked several times.

"Anita, please."

Cameron's voice snatched her from the past and back into their tiny apartment and back into her miserable circumstance. She tried to see through the midst gathering in her angry eyes. Her hands shook with rage as Cameron, apparently desperate to rid himself of her, jammed an ink pen into her palm. After several gasps and gulps for air, she was able to speak, "No, I will not sign them." Her head was moving quickly from side to side.

"Anita, you may be happy to torment your family for the rest of your life by using me, but I want to be with someone who loves me. This has been a long time coming, but I finally feel that I deserve something better, something real."

"I will not leave you, Cameron." She went over and sat in his lap. She wanted to use the touch, as her mother had instructed, which had been so successful in the past.

"I know what you're thinking, Anita. It won't work this time. I want, I need, more than this physical relationship."

She ignored him and moved her hands down his sides.

"Stop. I don't understand you. Don't you have any pride?" He shoved her into her own seat. "You have nothing to gain here. You don't love me and I ... I do not... I... can't love ...you..." He swallowed hard.

How she managed to stay in that chair, she didn't know. She didn't hear anything past the, "I do not love you." It cut like the razor-sharp edge of one of her father's samurai swords and it hurt worse.

"...continuing this farce..."

Was he still talking? Why? Hadn't she told him, no? She looked over to the sink where he was standing, pain etched across every inch of his face. She sat stunned, staring at him, through him.

"Just sign the papers, Anita. You and I both know you want to." Cameron bit his lip.

Was this some kind of test? She didn't want to, and if he had been paying any attention at all, he'd know she didn't want to.

"Still, if there was love…" He looked up and off as if imagining what might have been.

"Cameron, I do…"

"What?" his head snapped in her direction.

"I do… I do not wish to sign your papers." She struggled to stand. "… It's not true. I mean not right. Anyway, I can't. Yes, I can't sign. I am with child." She hadn't meant to say that, and it wasn't exactly true, but if it worked…

"You are?" He held on to the sink as if steadying himself. "You are having a baby, our baby…" He stared at her as if he was trying to make sense of it all. So was she. Finally he moved toward her, reaching for her. "My god, why didn't you tell me?" He grabbed her hands, pulling her to her feet. "I wondered why you were so tired all the time." He pulled her to his chest. "This changes everything."

Anita felt a glimmer of hope.

"We'll have to stay married, for the child." He held her away looking into her eyes as if this would make her understand better. "Anita, I'm so grateful. Our own child. The things we'll teach him, or her." He smiled. "We'll take him on the Manzanar Pilgrimage."

"What?" she questioned in a kind of fog.

"You know, the internment camps in California that the Japanese had to endure after World War II.

He's got to know his history. Many Japanese Americans go there yearly. Our child will have to go."

"Yes of course," she mumbled. "I hope we can wait till he walks."

Cameron smiled brilliantly. She had given him the one thing he wanted more than her love, perhaps more than God. A child. She'd won. She had him. So why did she feel more lonely and hurt than she ever had before?

"Anita, you did what!" Shelly snapped upon hearing of Anita's deceit.

Anita could see the look of shock on Shelly's face as she breezed into the store and started cleaning and talking as if she'd never missed a day of work. She had to talk to someone, and Shelly was the closest thing she had to a friend.

"I'll be the first to admit that Cameron has his issues," Shelly continued. "But he has been trying. My grandmother says he attends Mt. Prospect faithfully, and pretenders never last long there. It's obvious that he is doing something different with his life. And, Anita, it was so blatant how he felt about you.

Even Mark had to admit that Cameron's devotion to your marriage seemed sincere, and you know what a skeptic he is when it comes to anything regarding Cameron."

"Yes, seemed. He seemed sincere. What does your husband sense about my husband's feelings toward me these days?"

"Well…" Anita could feel Shelly hedging, trying to protect her feelings.

"You don't have to say it. Cameron tolerates me. He barely stands me."

"It's not that bad, Anita."

"It's not that good either."

"Mark's seen him from time to time at Mt. Prospect's mens' group. He said Cameron has more peace but is still struggling with something and around here he's been… But trapping him into staying with you, Anita. For what? You don't even like him…do you?"

"Well, I like being with him."

"What do you mean…sexually?"

"Yes, I like…I like the physicalness of him."

"Anita, sex is no basis for a marriage. And don't you still love Harold?"

"Harold…well, I find, I find myself —"

The newly installed door chime chirped as a tall Asian man walked in. "Harold?!" Anita squealed.

Anita felt queasy and had to hold onto the counter to maintain her balance.

"Are you all right?" Shelly was quick to ask, looking from her to Harold.

Anita nodded, pulled herself upright, and marched right past Harold and out the door. She looked back to see disappointment written all over Shelly's face. Probably thought that the very sight of Harold had caused her to swoon. It didn't. He was wearing Bernardo Bernier, that rich aromatic cologne he always wore and for some reason it made her sick to her stomach. She also knew Cameron would be home soon, and she didn't want to waste one moment she could be spending with her husband talking to Harold.

Anita walked across the living room floor and raised the window. She inhaled deeply. The fresh, sun-soaked air filled her lungs and a slick sensation rolled across her tongue. She could just about taste the salami from Nick's Deli on the corner. August had finally arrived and with it an early birthday present, her appetite returned.

Maybe she wouldn't have to tell Cameron about her hoax after all. She was swallowing TV dinners like she was a pig and marching blocks over to Dom's grocery to get large boxes of Jays chips. She'd ordered bad Chinese two times this week, licking her lips and putting the grease-stained cartons in the hall trash before Cameron got home. Every part of her body was starting to fill out and her stomach was even starting to round.

She felt a bit guilty. Last night Cameron came home with more books. He had one on child rearing and another on natural childbirth by Grantly Dick-Read. "Could that be his real name?" she joked pointing at the cover. They laughed together like they did in the beginning. "What are you doing?" she questioned blithely as Cameron lowered his mouth to her belly.

"Hello, Baby. Daddy can't wait to meet you." Her stomach tumbled and turned from her guilt. She felt awful. What would it do to him to know that she was pretending?

She needed to speak to the one person who knew most about these things, and the one person who could not bring herself to treat her badly. She needed her mother. So she'd risk it. She was going home. Mother would know what to do, and if her father didn't like it, too bad. What could he do, disinherit her? She laughed aloud imagining him standing tall in his traditional garb pointing his finger and saying, "Anita, I'll... why I'll..."

"Nothing!" she'd yell...in her mind of course. *Why had she obeyed him and stayed away,* she mused looking in the hall mirror combing and brushing her short hair with the silver metal set her mother gave her. She liked the way the beauty lady cut it, a straight line, a couple of inches below her ears. She squinted at her reflection. Her father's cheek line and nose peeked back at her. Maybe he'd be happy to see her. He wasn't going to whip her, as Shelly called spanking. The money was already taken away so there was nothing, absolutely nothing, he could do. She said it over and over, trying to convince herself. She fluffed her bangs. Perhaps she was as dull as Cameron intimated with his silence. She had, after all, been afraid of a man who clearly had no power left to wield over her.

Let's see, she thought, walking into their room and rambling through the clutter on his desk, always clutter. *Ah there you are.* She picked up the car keys and headed for the door. Hopefully she wouldn't crack up his little Jaguar. She hardly ever drove.

Cameron was on one of his walks. She didn't want to go. He was probably stalking some quaint neighborhood peering into shop windows for their "baby." "Anita, this would be so cute on our daughter." "Let's get these cute booties. Look they come in green and red and purple and pink." No, she just couldn't be part of that. She'd go see her parents and be home before he even knew she'd left.

Anita jumped into Cameron's Jaguar, squeezed the wheel, closed her eyes, and tried to remember what her father taught her. Clutch, break, gas. No, clutch, gas, break. Neutral, first, second. Oh, phoo, it couldn't be that hard. She yanked the stick while releasing the clutch and pressing the gas. There was a horrible screech, but she was off. She managed to get her window rolled down. The wind whipping her hair and the air stinging her cheeks made her feel wild. She ripped the gears from first to second to third then back. She didn't want to damage Cameron's car, but the thought of seeing her parents after so long a separation made her giddy. She really missed them. The speedometer went from 30 to 50 as she hurled through the city toward her family's home. The thought of racing to the two people who had all but given her up for dead made her laugh out loud.

Here we are. She patted her belly. *Pretend-baby and me.* "Hello Jothan!" she yelled at the gatehouse. "Don't just stare at me. I'm not a ghost."

He was clearly weighing his options, had likely been given strict orders not to admit her.

150

"Jothan, please. They want to see me." She poked her lower lip out and gave her best imitation of a sad sack. It must have worked because the gate opened and she rolled carefully up the circular driveway. She was glad to see Kim Kai at the bottom of the stairs. She took her arm and was surprised to find that she was totally exhausted after the first two steps.

Once at the top of the stairs, she studied her home. The frosty white exterior looked every bit the ice palace her husband proclaimed it to be. The large doors opened slowly as she entered. "Anita!" the familiar howl stopped her in her tracks. He was behind her. She'd never get to her mother at this rate. She pulled her shoulders back and turned to face her father's angry voice. As she readied herself for his reprimand his face softened.

"Daughter." He held out his hands. "You are..."

What! she wanted to yell. *I am what?* she threatened to spew. Instead, the threaded ropes, which hung from the ceiling, began to wiggle and melt. Her knees went weak. Dizziness overtook her.

Waking to the gentle mix of Orient meets the States, that was her bedroom, Anita focused on her mother standing, squeezing a wet cloth into her ornamented black-blue basin. "Husband, come quick she is awake," Akiko spouted. Anita was surprised to see her father standing by the fireplace where healing incense was lit. He rarely entered her "menagerie," as he called her room, and woman's sicknesses were of little concern to him. Easily contracted, easily overcome, he'd always say. Yet here he was moving to her bedside and stroking her hand no less. "Why didn't you tell us?"

More nonsense, she thought. All of this was so unlike him.

"Tell you what?" she almost swore.

"About your baby, Nita." Her mother sat on the side of the bed and stroked her forehead.

She moved her mother's hand aside. "What do you mean?" Anita asked through dry and parched lips.

"Anita, why didn't you tell us about this. Our grandchild," her father insisted, looking sad and happy all at once.

"Oh that. I've been using it as an excuse to hold on to... but how did you know about it?" As the words streamed out, Anita suddenly realized that there was no way they could know about her hoax, so they must be reacting to something else; maybe the way she...

"Mother..." She reached for Akiko, pulling her close, tears staining her face. "But I hardly have a belly."

"Daughter, you are just like I was with you." Akiko laid her hand on Anita's barely-there stomach.

"Anita." Her father finally smiled. "You look just like your mother did when she was carrying you. You are going to be a mother."

What a fool she'd been. She really was pregnant.

CHAPTER 16

Found?

Anita arrived early in the evening to Maple Drive. When she left her apartment, the chill of the 50-degree October day was hardly noticeable because the sun was so high and bright, but the temperature was dropping, fast. She pulled her collar up snugly and asked the taxi driver to wait. She wouldn't be long. Cameron didn't know about her driving his car and since that day she really hadn't wanted to try it again. But he was missing again. He had been several times to Wisconsin to work on a project for a new client or the church or something. She couldn't remember which. Not only did she have to share him with the church, but with someone or something in Wisconsin. At least she knew he wasn't there. He told her since the baby was close, he would be too. Close that is. But he still wasn't. There was still a part of him that he didn't share with her. If his desire for her had not returned, she might think he had another lover. *No, that couldn't be.* She silenced the thought.

This time, looking for him had brought her to Maple Drive. Perhaps there were answers to be found here. She had never visited the Schultz home though she had been right next door once with Shelly for a birthday dinner. She had not enjoyed it. Shelly's grandmother Rose, whose house she had visited, seemed to be able to see right into her and though she didn't say what she saw, the thought of her knowing made Anita feel strange. Of course, she didn't really know. How could she? But Anita skillfully avoided any more visits.

The elder Schultzes had become part of Cameron's life. She heard him speaking often to Mark's mother by phone. And she knew he occasionally visited them. Their home was an old stone Romanesque style house: huge pillars and large front windows facing three sides at once, quite beautiful really. Shelly used to talk about how the house had intimidated her when Mr. Schultz, her husband's father, was a rough, straightforward racist. My how times had changed. These days he was a rough, straightforward Christian. Anyway, she was only there to find her husband, not to visit with the house's inhabitants.

The heavy stone stairs reminded her of her own home. These were probably tailored for the giant men who lived and visited there, including her own husband. Anita rang the bell and waited impatiently for a response.

"Mrs. Schultz?"

"Yes, and you are Mrs. O'Neil." The woman had a welcoming but wary smile.

"I am. How did you know?" Anita stepped in, scanning the room for signs of Cameron.

Mrs. Schultz tilted her head and met her eyes. "Cameron has described you well. Come in. Make yourself comfortable."

Anita noted the immaculate furnishings and sighed. "Where is my husband?" She marched into the living room, immediately noticing an expertly refurbished recliner in the corner facing a TV. She knew it was re-covered because she recognized the fabric. Her mother, Akiko, had ordered it for her father's jewelry store just before she decided to start her own jewelry business. Such a small incestuous world they all lived in. "This is beautifully done." She meandered to the chair, lightly caressing the back-rest. "Where did you find such unique brads to do the nail work?"

"Mama Rose, I believe you know her. She helped me locate them, and your mother gave her this wonderful, rich fabric. I believe that the lushness of the material convinced my husband to let me cover his favorite chair. This chair is our centerpiece. The whole room is organized around it."

"I like it very much. You have a flair for decorating. I've never been much of a housekeeper...perhaps..." Anita cut herself off. She was there to find her husband not to explore her failings as a wife. She wasn't about to become a "Suzy-homemaker."

"You know, I wasn't a great homemaker myself. But Jacob is so neat, everything having a place and everything in it. I love him, and I want him to be happy so I've become good at it. He's still the best and sneaks behind me to tidy up from time to time; but I enjoy cleaning for him. It makes him happy, and that makes me happy."

"Humm," Anita paused, "Cameron is a very poor cleaner."

"Then you have a much harder job than I do."

"Not really," she said, intentionally flopping into Jacob's favorite chair.

"What do you mean?"

"The apartment is not orderly." Anita said, pulling up the lever on the side of the chair so she could lie back.

"What!" Irene snapped then calmed her voice, "I understand that you are putting in very little time at the store, and I know that Cameron works constantly. Why aren't you taking care of your home?"

She didn't wait for an answer just launched into her next statement, "You don't really understand love, do you?" She came around to face Anita with her hands on her hips. "Love is not just about desire. True love dictates a commitment and work."

"Work." Anita twisted in the chair sneering up at Irene, "You mean to tell me you have to work to love your man?"

"I mean to tell you, every day." Irene was near shouting, " And I'm not talking about physical work." Her hands were flying, "Yes, I desire Jacob and yes, I have deep feelings for him, but he gets on my nerves, he does things wrong, and occasionally I wish he'd go away."

"Oh, Mrs. Schultz," Anita hummed, "you are not being truthful with me." Anita released the chair lever and sat up straight. "Shelly has told me how much you and Mr. Schultz love each other. She said at times, you especially, cannot keep your hands to yourself."

"She said what?"

"Please don't tell her I said so. That was between me and her."

"Where it should have stayed…" Irene hissed.

"I'm sorry. What did you say, Mrs. Schultz?"

"Never mind." Irene walked away, "In spite of what you think you know to be true, there have been times that I needed a breather from my beloved and other things that I won't share with you…since I see what a great confidant you are…"

"Mrs. Schultz, you are mumbling."

"A habit I picked up from Jacob. Anyway, Anita, the point I was trying to make is that while love is a wonderful whimsical thing, it's not magic. When you marry someone, you believe not just that you love him, you believe in your love for him and in your commitment to him. And most of all you believe God is able to keep you two together. That is, with your cooperation. Do you see what I am saying?"

"Yes," Anita replied gritting her teeth and squinting, "It is not enough that I have to work to prove my worth, to have my own income. I also have to work to keep a man I didn't even want."

"Well, you certainly have your own way of looking at things." Irene blew hard and walked toward the front door. She opened it. "Maybe you should go and pray about it, see what God has to say."

"Oh, I don't believe in that. You must be thinking about my mother. She has recently started believing in your and Cameron's God."

"He is all of our God, Anita." She was holding the doorknob.

"I'll be the judge of that." Anita had heard enough. All this talk about God and commitment.

She loved Harold and he was a coward, unworthy of her, and Cameron had wanted her. These days all he was interested in was the baby she carried. Would he want her if there was no baby? She wanted him, but as Shelly so arrogantly said, that is not love. If only she could really understand him. If only someone could give her some guidance.

She pushed down on the arms of King Jacob's chair lifting herself to standing. Since she had not removed her coat, she made her way toward the door and out, not bothering to say goodbye to her hostess, and apparently not offending her in doing so since the woman didn't even pretend to care that she was leaving and hadn't bothered to offer any suggestions as to Cameron's whereabouts.

Irene grimaced as the young wife left. Anita hadn't found Cameron. She hadn't found him at all.

CHAPTER 17

Swept Away

Anita moved slowly through the kitchen with the broom in her hands. She didn't feel like sweeping, and she certainly wasn't about to drag that metal pail out of the closet, fill it with water, and mop. So she moped over to a kitchen chair and sat swinging her legs and looking at how messy everything was getting. Their lunch plates and glasses sat oily in the sink. A heavy pan, which Cameron used to fry trout, still smelled of fish.

"Why can't we keep this place any neater?" she said aloud.

"Why indeed," Cameron sneered from the couch.

"I saw that. If you were here, I'd do more. You are always gone. I can't believe that church has that much work. And they can't be paying you enough. How are you able to support us even in these meager surroundings?"

"Anita." He looked up from his notes. "In spite of your apparent disdain for me, and the fact that I'm getting really tired," he blew, "I'm trying. Something is telling me to hold on. Listen, it's not just us to think about. I want our child to have a family. My family life was horrible, and as bad as it was, things got worse for me when I lost my parents. You probably can't understand what I'm saying."

"I see. You think I'm dull. Just because I get nervous–*still, when I speak to you*– and lapse into my mother's broken English doesn't mean I don't understand."

"Anita." Cameron got up, ran his hands through his hair and pierced her with his clear green eyes. "You are ever seeing and not perceiving," he said pacing. "Ever hearing and not understanding. There is nothing wrong with your intelligence. There is something wrong with your heart. I'm not judging you. I was you."

The look of sympathy in his eyes when he stopped, clapped his hands together, then threw them up in exasperation infuriated her.

"You think you know so much." She got up from her chair and started stomping around on her fat and swollen feet. "You with your God and the God people." How did he know her, she wondered as she paced her own path through their small living room. She didn't even know herself.

She tried stomping hard. It was no use. The carpet muted the sound. Who was she? The overachieving daughter of Chuck and Akiko Kincaid, the rebellious, scheming brat who only wants her own way? Or something else? When had she become this person?

And what about him? Had he really become a good man, "a God man," or was he just another Cinderella coach soon to turn into a pumpkin? If she tried, could she be the woman that the "new" Cameron could respect?

She had never been more confused. One thing was for sure: Cameron was becoming lost to her. And she was becoming lost to herself. It seemed unfathomable to lose whatever part of Cameron she still held to a baby. Sure he was good to her, but she had gone from being defiled to being an infidel, an infidel! He hadn't said it, but it was in the way he looked at her, the "unbeliever." She was not going to be anyone's pity case, she wasn't.

Ah, there was still one thing left to get her husband's attention, one last thing to know where his loyalty lay.

"Cameron?" She stopped by the sink, put the rubber stopper in, and started the hot water running.

"Yes, Anita?" He had gone back to being hunched over his work, writing in his tablet and ignoring her.

"Harold is back."

Cameron sat up straight. His back was stiff.

"He'll be working at my father's Chicago office."

"And what has that to do with us!" He stabbed his pen into the table.

She wasn't sure where she was going with this, but she had his undivided attention, and it felt good. Was the old Cameron about to emerge? The strange thing is, just months ago they would have been a perfect match: perfect at conniving, perfect at making people pay. Admittedly, she had not always been this way, but she was proving to be good at it.

"Cameron." She really didn't need to call him again. His angry eyes never left her face. Did he know what she was about to say? She wasn't sure herself.

She removed her hands from the still steaming pile of dishes in the sink and sauntered over to his bookshelf. With hands still wet, she picked up their wedding picture.

A pudgy little man had snapped it with his camera as they exited the state building. Cameron quickly scribbled out their address so he could mail it to them when he developed it.

"You must be the happiest man alive." He had slapped Cameron on the back. Cameron tried to smile.

The picture showed her wearing a plain black knee-length dress and Cameron with a white dress shirt and black pants. His smart black suit coat with formal tie and vest came off—along with his bright smile—when she removed her coat to reveal her dull, everyday-dress. She did feel bad about that. Perhaps a more festive dress would have been appropriate. They had walked silently into the judge's chambers. Seemed she just couldn't stop herself from hurting him. She wasn't a sadist, and if she really believed he loved her...

"I want to see him," she spat at Cameron.

"Stop it!"

"What?"

"I wasn't talking to you—"

"Well, we're the only ones here," she sniped.

"Anita, what are you saying? You are married and carrying my child. It's not proper for you to go off cavorting with your former lover."

"He was not...yes, he... he is my..." Anita was overtaken by the urge to make Cameron notice her. Cameron's head was already shaking, "no," but she was undeterred. "Yes, Harold is my former lover and not too former at that. This is not your..."

Anita was packed into the car so fast it made her head spin. Cameron had yanked her clothes from hangers and swept her toiletries into a brown paper bag faster than the tornado in Oz pulled up Dorothy's house. Next came the quickest drive she had ever experienced to her parents' suburban home. She saw gray, frost, sunlight, store signs too blurred to read, and faces too fast to make out, all pass by in what felt like mere seconds. Her heart leaped and her baby was trying to get out. They must have broken the barrier of sound upon leaving Cameron's apartment. And the lights, green, yellow, red, all meant the same thing: get this witch home as fast as possible. As they rounded the sleet-smeared driveway on the two side tires of Cameron's black Jaguar, she prayed for her life. Then the car drop-stopped. "Get out!"

"Cam-eeeron, may I speak?" she slurred like a barroom broad.

"GET OUT!" he roared, face beet-red and veins popping from his temples. She had his attention. He ripped her suitcases from the trunk and flung them on the massive stairs that led to the frosty white castle that she knew as home. Next, her tall, well-built man lunged for the door where she sat too frozen to move. He yanked it open and held out his hand to her. She took it, ready to also take whatever abuse he would spew her way. He closed his hand around hers and tugged gently. She squeezed her eyes shut, refusing to see the pain she had written on his face. To her surprise he released her. There was no more anger, no scorn, no sorrow, nothing. Their fingers unwound, slowly and deliberately. His car sped away as she lumbered to the stairs.

Walking slowly, she looked up to see Clyde already outside. He made no move to assist her. Instead he turned and pumped the great gold knocker on one of the doors. A servant, who Anita did not know, opened it. No one helped her up the stairs, so she left her suitcases below. As soon as she entered, her mother approached, looked at her, and simply asked, "Nita, what have you done this time?"

Cameron knew he should get past the gatehouse before he let loose, but control had apparently forgotten his old friend Cam. As soon as the castle doors closed on Anita, he howled. Then he put the car in gear and was sure he had popped a wheelie racing over the icy gardens and glancing the iron fence. He couldn't see anymore, so he cried. He cried bitter, he cried long. He cried for all the women he had wronged: Sally who he stood up because Libby had bigger breasts; Libby who he stood up because Anita said yes; he cried for beautiful Jessie who developed a limp as a result of a car accident, so he suddenly could not be located for their weekly "appointment." He cried for Carol, Grace, and Felicia. He cried for his mother whom he was too weak to save, and he cried for his father who could no longer be bothered to see his son. He cried for every twist he should have turned and for every tear he should have shed long ago, and finally he cried for the son or daughter who no longer existed and for the wife who never did. And just before his chest heaved one last long time, he cried for the life he could no longer bear to live.

"Akiko, is that Anita?" his voice sounded from a distance.

"Yes, Father, it is me. Am I still not welcome here?" Her voice seemed to echo off the cavernous walls. Anita's father came forward looking every bit his imposing, powerful self. He was wearing his forest green smoking jacket and an inscrutable look on his face. Toting a pipe, which he had just lit, he waved the match smoke away with a flick of his wrist but said not a word.

"Well, Father, am I welcome?" Anita watched the smoke sail into the silent emptiness.

"That depends, daughter. Tell me, where is your husband, and what, my child, have you done this time?"

What had she done? And why did both her parents think she had done some big monstrous horrible thing? With her still full suitcases, Anita arrived at the home of Shelly and Mark Schultz, and she would not be there if she could think of any place else in the world to be.

"But Father, where shall I go..," she had asked.

"Home!" he roared. No sympathy.

Anita wiped the frosty-crisp tears from her cheeks. To tell Shelly any version of what she had done would bring quick and explosive retribution. Not that she had ever seen Shelly mad or even indignant, but she was a Christian and Anita just knew that she would judge her. After all, isn't that what they did?

The small brick building where Shelly lived was well-kept. It looked like the snow right in front of the building had been shoveled, though she had to get there. Anita strode up the long sidewalk that led to the outside door. She leaned up against it. She had arrived with great difficulty, supporting a belly full of a seven-month-old baby and a platter full of her mother's finest delicacies. She had gathered as much food as she could while she was telling her story and before her father called her an insolent little fraud and threw her out. He looked extremely hurt as he hurled the words with ferocity that didn't become even him. Her mother kept interjecting, "He doesn't mean that, Nita."

"Of course I do," he countered, hands flying to punctuate his words. "She was always spoiled, but compliant and I dare say caring and capable of compassion. I wasn't sure if I was too late to avoid Harold's influence on her. Perhaps this is who she truly is. But the person who would intentionally disgrace an honorable man is no—"

"Chuck!" her mom had yelped in time to keep her father from saying a dreaded, can't-take-it-back-ever statement. Anita knew she would forgive him—someday—but would he have been able to forgive himself? One thing nagged at her though. Did her father actually mean to call Cameron honorable?

The cab driver who whisked her from her father's home simply took her two heavy Valencia bags out of his trunk and laid them on the curb, *Valencia*, mind you. He tipped his yellow cap in her direction and jumped back into his yellow cab like he had been promoted to fire marshal and a hotel full of homeless children was aflame down the block. He didn't bother to ask this balloon-of-a-woman if she needed any assistance to the door.

Could everyone see her evil? With no help, she ambled along, dragging one suitcase, then the other, making wide suitcase-shaped patterns through the snow on the public sidewalk. Finally, both bags rested next to her at the door.

"Yes, who's there?" Anita felt more tears well in her eyes at the sound of Shelly's voice echoing sweetly through the intercom.

Shelly, please, please be as nice as I think you are. "It's me, Shelly. Anita."

"Anita?"

Somehow she had managed to hold the door open tugging one suitcase over the threshold then pulling the second as it scratched and scraped the ground, huffing more heavily with the second which had to be as heavy as she was. This couldn't be good for her or the baby. *God help me if I lose the one person in this world who may actually be able to love me and forgive me for what I've done.* "Yes, it's me. Can I please come up, and can you send Mark down?"

"Brother Schultz, it was my job to keep her alive." Rumpled, wet, and fidgeting, Cameron sat on the edge of Jake's favorite chair wailing about God knows what. "I failed, I was weak, help me please. God this is crazy, I'm never going to cry again. It's like I opened the flood gate and can't get it closed." He was shoving the palms of his hands into his eyes.

"It's okay, son, everybody cries, sometimes." Jake turned, mumbling, "I, for one, have never seen so many tears—"

"Sir?"

"Call me Jake. And it's okay, most of us don't have the stuff to deal with that you do."

"It was years ago, Brother Jake, I was on the couch trying to rest. My mother was lying on her bed, twisting and turning."

"Um humm, Renie, can you get in here? Cameron needs to tell you the rest of his story. Quick, honey, I think this is your area."

Jake jumped from the chair where he was sitting near Cameron, went to the kitchen entryway, and looked longingly for his wife. "Renie, we need you in here!"

"Coming, Jacob, just letting Mary out the back door." She swept into the room, hand flying immediately to her face. "I thought you said Cameron was here?" she whispered, discretely holding her nose.

Jake gave a quick head nod in the general direction of the "stranger."

"Cameron?" she questioned. She hurried to the chair next to their unrecognizable friend.

"Dear-heart, what's wrong? Your hair's all matted and your clothes—" She touched his cheek. "Please tell me, what's going on?"

"Can I leave, Honey?" her husband's heavy hand was on her shoulder.

"Yes, Jacob, but stay close. We may need you."

"You think I'm going to break down, don't you?" Cameron sat up, trying to resurrect his shield.

"Cameron." Jake stopped in the doorframe. "What we think is not important. It's what you think. Mark's told us some about you before you came to us: the lies, the schemes, the women. Try to trust God's love. It's okay for the old Cameron to break down, to fall away. Satan has kept you in a prison for a long time, making you think that you could only be good by being the last man standing, and when you no longer agreed with him, when he saw he was losing his grip, he doubled his attack."

"The voices?"

"Yes, can you think of anything that gave the Devil the ability to taunt you like this?"

Cameron thought back to the evening Mark bloodied his lip. "Yes. I hope this is okay to talk about, but it was the night I took Shelly out, and Mark came to inquire."

Jake nodded his consent for Cameron to continue.

"Well, Shelly answered the late night knock on the door. It was Mark. She immediately started telling him how terrible he looked."

Jake snorted.

"Your son must have made a last minute decision to check on Shelly, and when he found me there he lost control."

"Mark?"

"Yes Mark."

"You musta' had it coming."

"Jacob!" Irene spouted giving her husband a sideways glance.

"I was touching her."

"I knew it."

"Jacob, please leave. We'll call if we need you. Go on, son, you can tell us anything."

"I taunted Mark by blowing on Shelly's hair, then I put my hand on her hip. She was apparently too mad at him to notice. Donna, Shelly's friend, was squealing from somewhere in the apartment. She wanted to know what all the loud talking was about. I'll never forget it. When Shelly turned to respond, Mark took his shot. I never had a chance to react. It

hurt, but that didn't matter. I was amused at first…
that I'd gotten to him. My lip was wet, so I touched
it. The blood was all over me."

"All over 'im? He's hysterical, Irene." Jake yelped
from his corner.

"Shelly saw my lip bleeding and slammed the
door on your son, sorry. I wanted to savor my victory,
but I could feel old memories surfacing, memories
that I had buried. It was the blood on my hands…
anyway, when she escorted me to the table and started to carefully put soothing cloths to my mouth—
her nursing was so tender—"

"Uh um," Jake piped again from the corner.

"Go ahead, Cameron." Irene turned to glare at
Jake. He glared right back.

"Her sincerity, it was deep and the honesty of her
touch—"

"That's enough, Renie," Jake warned.

"Cameron, let's get right to what's troubling you."

Cameron stopped, a little embarrassed about
gushing over their daughter-in-law. His head
jerked suddenly as if someone had called from
his past. "Her wrists, Sister Irene." He was holding both of Irene's hands and searching her arms.
"When I woke, the television was fuzzy. It was after
midnight."

"He better not be talking 'bout Shelly's place," Jake said, pacing, his big arms folded across his chest.

"He's... not." Irene whined, wincing at the pain of Cameron gripping her wrists so tightly.

Jake rushed over to pry Cameron's fingers loose.

"I tried to stay up until my father got home. Really, I did, but I fell asleep. I wasn't supposed to, and when I got up I knew something was wrong. She was too quiet."

"Did he kill somebody?" Jake whispered.

Irene shrugged.

"I ran to her room, and she was lying there, her eyes open and void. Her arms were stretched out, but they were not tied. He sometimes tied them."

"Your father?"

"One wrist was cut a little, the other wide open. There was blood everywhere. I grabbed both her wrists, cupping my hands over the raw slits. I was trying to hold them together. I cried for someone to help me. When every tear was gone and there was nothing left, my father appeared in the doorway. He was slumped there, heaving frantically. His trench coat was hanging off his shoulders and his briefcase dangled limp from his fingers. When he finally spoke, he yelled, 'Cameron, what have you done?!'"

Cameron's hair was long and dirty. He was wearing days-old clothing, unwashed, and wrinkled. Weary and worn, he looked up at his hosts expecting to find the condemnation he always did whenever he allowed himself to be truly known. He was beaten and ready… ready to just give up.

"We've got to call Cameron, now!" Mark hissed, pulling his wife into their crowded pantry. "It's been weeks. We've got our own baby to care for."

"Can't we be a little sympathetic? Her baby's not here yet, Honey." Shelly whispered.

Mark squinted. "Thank God for that. She's a bigger baby than L.J. ever was. At least he's feeding himself. Did she tell you what happened? What about her parents? Does she have any other relatives, any real friends? Why doesn't Cameron come for her?" Shelly opened her mouth to speak. "Don't answer that, it doesn't matter, he needs to come for his wife." Mark was getting louder and pointing. "I swear, if she stays any longer—"

Shelly shushed her husband and pulled him by the wrist out of earshot, which was no easy task; he was taller than Cameron and much wider. "What do you want me to do? She's all alone."

"You... mean... she's... a...li...e...na...ted," his syncopated whisper was hardly subtle, "everyone who could possibly care about her, and I don't understand who could."

Anita bit her lip. Why was Mark so mad? All she was doing was sitting on the sofa with her feet up. "Shelly, I'm cold. Can you bring me something warm to drink? And maybe Mark wouldn't mind going out for tempura. It's not as good as my mother makes, but I have such a craving."

"Just a minute, suga'-plum-fairy."

Anita had thought that was Mark's pet name for her, but, this time, she could just about see him gritting his teeth as he strained out the words. She knew his patience was gone. He had his own wife and baby to take care of.

Despite her actions lately, she was not an ignorant woman. She heaved a huge sigh. Had her desire to hurt her father driven her to destroy everything she ever wanted? She looked toward the terrace, and by the glow of the floor light bouncing off the sliding glass doors, she could see violent tears running down her cheeks. "Shelly, please come, Shelly..." Her legs were flailing, and she was scratching the couch arm of their nice leather sofa.

"Anita, calm down." Suddenly Mark and Shelly were sitting on either side of her. She was shaking so frantically that she became scared. They both cradled her, and all she could think of was how badly she wanted her Cameroon's arms about her. She was hiccupping and digging her fists into her eyes. "Help me. Please, help me." She clutched both their thighs. "I've been such a child. I've destroyed everything."

"It's not too late," Mark inserted, patting her hand, hard. "We can take you home and surprise Cameron."

"He's not home. I've called over and over again."

"Then where is he?" Mark squealed uncharacteristically.

"Honey," Shelly cautioned, "why don't you go get Anita that tea and let me talk to her."

"Shelly," Anita managed, after more simpering. "I'm going home."

Mark Flintstone-skidded back into the room, tea sloshing over the edge of a small cup. "I'll get your bags."

Home sweet home. Not really, Anita thought, as she walked around her small apartment dusting shelves and knocking down cobwebs. Where was Cameron? Was he ok? *Don't think of him, he's not your problem,*

leave him to his God; that's all he talks about, or cares about anymore.

"Come home, Nita," her mother whined daily, worried about her being alone and pregnant.

"It's alright, daughter," her father had softened. He called her regularly, begging her to come home as well. But she could not. They visited and she allowed it, but to admit failure and run to mommy and daddy…no not that.

Before she could let Cameron go, she had some things to say, and he was going to hear it if she had to wait until…when? *Don't think about it, just cook and clean; keep busy. Cameron will not recognize the place when he gets home.* She had committed herself to getting their home ready for his return. He would come back to her. He had to. She had purchased new bedding and straightened up the bedroom, putting everything in its place. As soon as she finished dusting, she'd put the bright blue throw on the hard front couch along with some new softer cushions. Maybe she could have done some of this before. No matter, she was finally doing it and…what's this? Another one of his books pushed under the stiff old cushion. She tossed the tablet full of writing on the table. It opened to a warning…something about reading other people's inner thoughts. What a silly man… there were no secrets between husband and wife.

Was she still his wife? If she was unfaithful, what did that make her?

Being grown up was too complicated. No wonder she had avoided it all these twenty-four years. She might not be a wife, but her tight and swollen belly reminded her she was about to be a mother. She thought about this, as she opened and began to read the mystery pages before her. If he didn't want anyone to see his stuff, he should not be such a slob.

The thought of him not thinking she'd find it because she never cleaned never crossed her mind.

CHAPTER 18

Visitors...

Despite wearing sunglasses, the sun shone so bright Cameron had to shield his eyes to take in the view. He still marveled at the trees leaning in response to the clear and heavy ice bending them over. The frosted pines, like Christmas statues, provided fleeting respite from the unyielding winds burning the small amount of his skin left exposed around his cheeks and in the gaps between his sleeves and gloves as he went crunching through the ice-coated ground and slicing through the crisp cold air which had become his solace. It was here he communed with himself, nature, and most importantly, God. His bread-crumb analogy had held true; little by little God was leading him, first to the church, then to the woods, and to an understanding of who he was in God's sight.

As Pastor Marvin said: if you want to know how a car works, what it can do, and how to fix it, you consult the manufacturer and the manual. He had thought it a clunky analogy, but God was speaking to him through his Word and in prayer. He'd been praying aloud and often. There were times he felt he might go into that other realm that some of the saints talked about.

The voice was gone. Mr. Schultz, or Brother Jake—as he was trying to get used to calling him—had said, "It has been cast out. But listen, son," he cautioned, "it will try to get back in. You've done the hard work. Now you have to keep it out."

"But how?" he had asked.

"By staying like this with God," the elder Schultz had said, doing the two finger eye-to-eye gesture. "If you and God see eye-to-eye, the Devil won't have an inch of room to get back in. And that means seeing yourself the way God sees you, the way I've come to see you: a man full of possibilities. Good ones." Seems God had brought him here to learn who they both were. He'd been gone from Chicago over a month, only keeping in touch with Pastor Marvin by phone when he went into town for groceries. He didn't drive himself. His sporty Jaguar could no longer make the trip. The snow and ice had proved too much and, given the impending weather, it was simply time to hunker down and stay in.

He still missed her; he was loath to admit. And the thought of the baby continued to bring pain and anger. He imagined himself and Anita raising their son or daughter. He thought she'd have Anita's dark hair and her unusual sense of humor. He thought his son would be the boy he would have been had not tragedy and neglect made his soul vulnerable to death and destruction. He and Anita would have raised him to be a good man who knew God and cared about people. He would have had enough, and most importantly he would have had love.

It wasn't to be. He had been a fool. Anita wasn't the woman of his dreams. She was a nightmare: a selfish, hateful girl. It was the enemy who had clouded his vision and made him see something that wasn't there. Only, even at his most vulnerable, he had always been able to see "good." He knew because he avoided it like the plague. Just his luck to be off base when it counted most. One thing this adventure had shown him was that there was "good" in him and what he lacked, God would make up. At least that's how he thought it worked. God would help him to forgive Anita and not kill Harold, then he'd get on with life and start over. He peered up between the ice-coated evergreens into the brilliant sunlight and said a silent prayer for Anita and her unborn child.

Her feet had never been so cold. Anita slipped and skidded up the uneven walkway in front of the rough wooden cabin. Canny Konley, who had driven her from the bus depot, whizzed past her twice carrying her large brown Louis Vuitton and smaller Valencia suitcases like he was in a relay race. She placed her leather-gloved hand on her side and tried to massage away the twinge in her lower back, which still ached from the bus ride to Anderson, Wisconsin.

She had ridden sideways most of the way, attempting to keep her pregnant belly from bumping the seat in front of her as she awoke to a groggy, cotton-mouthed, stop. "No more departures today, ladies and gents. Thanks for traveling with Grey's Bus Company." As soon as she got down from the bottom step, with the driver's help, cold hulking flakes, like small fists warning her to stay away, started pounding.

"What you doin', lady?" a towering stranger, wearing an orange and green hooded overcoat, asked as he rammed into her while she fumbled through her purse searching for the tablet page.

"I'm looking for the livery service," she had said shaking and trying to fit under a store awning.

"Livery, that some kind of China word?" he quipped, thick and slow. She tamped down her anger. He might be able to assist her. Everyone else hurried to their cars or the local bus stop. The lights

in the depot were switching off, so ignoring his igno-
rance only made sense.

"No Mister...er, can I have your name?"

"Konley, Canny Konley. I came to pick up my
brother. Guess he missed the bus. So what's a lady
of your refined styling doing in a place like this and
what's this livery you talkin' 'bout?"

"I'm h..ere to see my hus...band," she hissed
through chattering teeth. "I'm Japanese, and I'm
looking for the livery, some kind of driving service."
Pulling her lapel across her chest, she continued,
"Maybe a cab or limo—"

"Limo," he gasped as if trying to catch his breath,
"boy, are you in the wrong place. And what kind of
man you got having you out here in this weather?"

"My husband doesn't know I'm here. It's, it's kind
of a surprise."

"A big one, I'd guess by the size of you." He
slapped his leg, guffawing at his own joke.

"Listen, Mr. Konrey."

"That's Konley."

"Mr. Konrey, do you know where I can get a car
and a driver?"

"Ain't no cabby in this town, Miss. Sometimes Jeb
Steward drives people around for money, but he's
out of town visiting his mom up north."

"More up north than this?" Anita mumbled.

"What's that?"

"Can you help then?"

"I don't know, Miss. I'm on a schedule, supposed to pick up my brother and get back out to the farm to help my father before the weather sets in."

"I heard the radio say it will be bad."

"Bad! Lady, up here when it snows, bad ain't the word. Where you trying to go?"

"Here?" she said, pointing at the precise script on the bottom of a drawing of a smallish log cabin neatly nestled among tall trees. It had a Lincoln-Log-like red wood fence all around it. All she could think was: what would a man like Cameron ever be doing at a place like this? She could only hope he actually was there.

"I'd like to help you, Miss, but this is way out of the way and my brother..."

Anita hated herself for what she did next, but she felt it was her only recourse. "Please, sir," she sniffled pulling a handkerchief from her leather pocket book and poking at her eyes. "My husband is there, and I'm all alone."

"I don't know," the big moose groused and turned away.

"Ok then," Anita huffed digging deeper into her pocket book. She rounded him. "What about this? Will you do it for this?" She flapped a crisp fifty-dollar bill at his face.

"Yes Ma'am!" he howled, then lowered his head. "My father will be more understandin' when I show him this," he simpered, looking away.

"It's okay. I understand demanding fathers. Where's your car please?"

Canny told her to wait right there, which to her was nowhere in this little bit of a town. The wind whipped her hair and stung her face. It was getting colder, and the snow was turning into something else. "Clang, screech, pop, plop, sssss," it came, the big green rust-mold machine. Side-to-side, her head started shaking involuntarily. "I…I can't."

"We made a deal, Miss. I'm here ready to take you where you wanna go. She don't look like much, but these big wheels'll take you anywhere in these parts." He continued.

She was still shaking her head, "no," as she felt his arm under hers hefting her into the passenger side.

After the first few bangs, she actually nodded in his rattling trap of a truck, which in addition to the mold, stank of animal scent mixed with… she didn't even want to guess. She remembered waking to harsh thumps and thuds as the truck jerked away from slick curbs. She closed her eyes tighter as she noticed the sheets of ice mounting on the windshield. She'd give Cameron a piece of her mind if she lived to complain about his choice of retreat. She pushed away thoughts of the possibility of him not being at the cabin at all.

After about forty minutes, twenty bumps, ten bounces, three repeats of the address, and two checks on the sketch, something resembling Cameron's drawing loomed in the distance. Luckily the address was in big black letters on a support post at the entry, which was being pelted with hard flecks of icy snow. In his drawing, a beautiful fence surrounded the place. In actuality, only one half of the cabin sported a fence. On the other side, under a heavy black cloak, lay a pile of logs stacked into a miniature mountain. The cabin was even smaller than it looked in Cameron's drawing, if that were possible. She could only imagine what kind of mess there must be on the inside. Cameron was not a good housekeeper, and she was sure these rustic surroundings had not improved his skills.

Canny Konley was no gentleman; after he dumped her luggage at the door, he gave her a quick nod, skated back to his horrible green box on wheels and snaked his way down the quickly disappearing, ice-coated roadway. She did not see Cameron's car. She was alone. God, she hoped not.

Anita knocked. Nothing. Then she pushed against the door, which did not give. Pulling her itchy wool coat about her prickly ears, her arms, upper body, and hands began shaking uncontrollably. Then the tears came in earnest. She sat atop her suitcase, an icy film clouding her view.

"Oh God," she gulped. A shrill wind answered her call. "Thanks for nothing!" she howled, hands flying to protect her face. *The one time I decide to pray and their God sends the tornado to finish me off. See if I ever...* A mighty gust shoved her. Jumping to her feet, she whirled toward the door fumbling for the handle. This time it opened instantly.

She hurried back out to pull her suitcases over the obscenely raised-threshold that guarded the cabin door as the tiny sheets of ice covering her eyes melted to reveal that she was having a delusion of epic proportions, as Cameron might put it. When her vision cleared, a wondrous sight was unveiled. A large red and yellow plaid couch sat nicely facing a huge mouthed fireplace. An oak table without a hint of clutter stood at arm's length from it. There were overstuffed chairs one on either side of the couch and two smallish tables in the background, one sporting artificial flowers and the other a dish filled with hard candy. As soon as her eyes lighted upon it, her hungry hands followed. Her husband had turned into a perfect housekeeper. Perhaps being without her was good. What if... her mind whirred.

What if this isn't his place at all? Or... Or what if there is a woman here keeping his place nice? Hot bile burned Anita's throat as she jammed her palms into her eyes, willing herself not to cry again.

Cameron had first come to the cabin to meet with a prospective client who was thinking of turning it and the surrounding area into a women's retreat center or "something." This client was going to hire Dobbs, Schultz & Brandon to advertise the location and the services the retreat would offer. Before Cameron could get out of his vehicle, Mr. Norm Lier, a thin, twittering man, was rattling, "It's a wash. She's done it to me again." He pounded on the hood of his car with his fist and kicked at the newly budding grass. "This was my wife's idea, and she's already moved on to something else. Do you know what they call men like me?"

"Uxorious."

"What? Please tell me you speak English."

Cameron nodded.

"Sorry you came here for nothing." Lier paced waving his arms frantically. "Looks like I won't need you fellas after all. I'm done with her schemes. Do you know any realtors? It's going on the market tomorrow!"

Before Cameron could answer, Lier jumped in his DeVille and drove away, leaving him to ponder taking on the six-hour drive back to Chicago. No way. He was exhausted. He was spending the night. Two days later, Cameron called Mr. Lier with an offer, "Sell me the property. No one needs to know you've had another failed venture." Cameron always had a nose for business. But this country cabin was sort of a joke. He didn't really know why he made the offer, but Lier immediately retorted, "Keep your mouth shut, and you've got a deal. What do you want to pay?'

His next weekend off, Cameron moved a bunch of necessities up as well as some nonperishable food. He also found a local resident to stop by the place from time to time to make sure it was still standing. He didn't know what might need to be done when the cabin was unoccupied, but Dan Newberry, his nearest neighbor, assured him that this was a necessity. Come to think of it, this might be the only time he had actually been duped. He smiled thinking of the possibility. That is, if he didn't count Anita. The smile disappeared.

Cameron heaved the heavy door that opened to his large wooden kitchen at the back of the cabin. He'd left the fresh meat on the back porch and put the fruits and vegetables just inside the door. Sam, a neighbor who thought he'd stop by to see who had moved into the cabin, had driven him to town for a quick shopping trip and dropped him back home an hour ago. For some reason, he needed to walk the property this evening before settling in. He was glad he did, because by the look of things no one would be getting out or in for days. He walked over to his stand-alone freezer and began putting away brown paper wrapped packages of fresh chicken, lean steak, hamburger, and bone-in pork chops. He was sorry his mind had wandered to Anita, because he could almost smell her scent as he put the milk, butter, and enough frozen boxes of Birdseye vegetables to feed a small army into his newly purchased refrigerator, *It had been over a month since he'd seen her. Haruto's baby should just be born.*

What made him buy so much? He thought, as he roamed his long stretched-out kitchen putting away detergent, first aid supplies, and more towels. Earlier this week he had purchased more firewood. Enough to last the entire winter, he laughed to himself. Maybe he was never going home.

After the grocery was put away, he returned to the back porch, walked out by the shed where his car was housed and made sure the extra wood outside was securely covered by a tarp.

Stand still, he thought, as soothing soft snow blanketed his cheeks. No more Anita. No more ad agency. He was home. He was at peace. God had favored him. It was a long time coming. "Thank you, Lord," he whispered into the mist.

Today he could even think about his childhood without **ITs** power over him...

After his mother was gone, he waited. Long lonely days walking around the apartment, washing one dish and one glass. He used the pointed end of the bottle opener to gouge triangles around the circumference of his tin cans to get to the Campbell's soups, the peas and carrots, the string beans, and the corn until there was nothing left. It wasn't unusual to be left in the apartment for two days but then his mother was with him. She was gone and he was alone, sitting, staring at the bed where she laid, arms splayed, eyes open. A week passed. There was no more food. Where was his dad?

Hungry, confused and scared, he meandered down the hall and down the stairs to the one place where the door was always open. Miss Mildred was sitting in her living room entertaining a guest.

"Cameron, come in child," she said as he stood simpering in the entry. "You look horrible," she hummed. "I'm so

sorry about your mother. I haven't seen you or David for days."

Cameron remembered feeling so little and scared. He stood before the only other grown-up he knew well, hoping she would help him in some way.

"Where is that handsome father of yours?"

He shrugged pitifully.

"Look at you," Mildred said with her hands on his arms spinning him this way and that. "All skin and bones. And have you been crying?"

Her apartment was all red, black, and lacy, closed in. The scent wafted between sweet and rank-sour.

"It's been a week, Miss Mildred. My dad must have had an accident. I don't know where he is."

"Don't worry, cutie." She rolled around in her chair, making room for him. "You are such a handsome boy." She curled her long finger down the side of his face. "Umphh." Shimmying her milky white shoulders caused her blouse to fall open. His neck jutted forward. He had never seen breasts before. "Oops." Her hand flew to her pooched ruff lips. She tickled her eyebrows up one side then down on the other. Mr. Fred looked from Mildred to him and then doubled over laughing. He had laughed too. The nervous laugh of a ten-year-old not knowing what was funny. Mildred pulled him to her and hugged him hard. "You can stay with me until David comes back," she smiled broadly.

His father never came back. Cameron had become her son, so she taught him her trade. Rubbing the clients' feet, massaging their shoulders, conversing with them about anything and everything, flattering them and generally doing whatever gave them pleasure. For the women, he had no limits. It wasn't until Mildred tried to "introduce" him to Jeff, a forty-year-old man, that he bolted. At sixteen, he fully understood the power of his looks and how to work the ladies. He could get whatever he wanted: down payments on cars, places to live, and even a college education of sorts.

He never really went. Sleeping on college campuses in their libraries and in their bathrooms, he "audited" a few classes and read all the books, then he had one of his well-heeled-connected women get him "official" transcripts, diplomas and certifications from little-known, mostly foreign institutions. Not that he needed them. As soon as he demonstrated his natural ability to cajole and manipulate, the only real qualities needed in advertising, he was on his way.

He was certain he would have ruled that realm if it had not been for Mark. On his next visit to Chicago, he'd actually make time to thank him. When Mark punched him in the mouth and he reached for the wound, the blood ran down his hand causing him to relive his mother's death. That was the day **IT** came screaming back, unrepressed and uncontrolled. But this time when it reared its ugly head, it heralded its own death. The demonic oppression was over. The tormenter that cursed God and mastered him was no longer in control.

The end of **IT**s life was the beginning of his own. **IT** had to be fully established to be fully routted.

That's what Mama Rose said when she came over to help the Shultz's revive him. It had been about two weeks after he'd left Anita with her family...

"Get in here Rose. Boy's been like this for over an hour." He could hear Jake Schultz's proclamation, yet he could not defend himself or utter a word. It was like there was a literal cloth tied around his mouth and frazzled ropes burning his arms and legs into place.

"An hour, you say?" Rose responded.

"That's what I said. I wanted to call an ambulance but Renie said we should call you first."

"He didn't respond to you and Irene?"

"Rose," Jake's voice had been loud and impatient, *"would you be standing here if he did?"*

Rose sighed a loud humph and pulled up a chair. That beautiful old black woman pressed her strong oil-anointed hands to his temples, called on the name of Jesus and began to do battle with the Devil. *"Go, you haughty, manipulative, spirit of arrogance and pride. In the name of Jesus,*

I command you." Then she proceeded to unstrap unseen buckles down the side of his body, three of them. The middle was the most difficult to unlatch, the one around his heart. Then suddenly, without warning, something...IT started to lift. Like a great weight, it began to rise. He sat up.

"Son, the spirit is gone," Rose proclaimed.

He shook his head.

"And when it comes back to challenge you..."

Back! He wanted to scream, but he could not speak.

"You will have to hold your ground. Do you understand?"

He didn't, and he couldn't open his mouth to say so.

She stared at him for a cold hard minute then cried out, "Oh you are a stubborn one. Jake, Irene, get over here. Jake, put your hand here."

He felt the heavy thud of Jake's hand on his abdomen as the big man kneeled to attach it.

"Irene, here and here." Mrs. Schultz's steady right palm pressed his chest while her other hand rested on his head.

Again Mama Rose unbuckled an invisible strap, the one that covered his mouth. "I adjure you, you deaf and dumb spirit, by the blood of Jesus, come out!" She yanked hard. He felt it literally and spiritually.

"Thank you. Thank you," he gasped, engulfing the entire group for a grateful lingering hug. That's when he caught a glimpse of another man in the hall, shaggy, unkempt. He didn't realize he was staring at himself in the *mirror. Then came the smell. It pricked his nostrils: rancid unwashed human. Again, him. "I'm sorry," he said pushing them gently back.*

"So are—" Jake had started to say, when Irene cut him off.

"Brother Cameron, there is nothing to be sorry about. We love you. We ALL love you." She glared at her husband.

"Of course we do," Jake said bounding to his feet. "Son, we have an extra room and a bath up stairs."

Sister Schultz grunted.

"I mean a bathroom," he corrected. "We have an extra room with a bathroom attached. You're welcome to stay awhile, get yourself together." He tapered off, "Clean up..."

Cameron remembered gently kissing Mama Rose's hands, then Irene's. They were still near. He approached Mr. Schultz who stepped back and waved him toward the stairs.

He had been so pitiful. To this day he wondered if he had been their worst case.

That all seemed so long ago. Bringing his thoughts back to Wisconsin, he looked up. "Thank you, Lord." He smiled into the snow before it turned into ferocious barbs pelting and threatening to pierce his face. *Time to go in.*

Cameron pushed on the heavy wooden door and wiped his boots several times on the mat lying beyond the back threshold. The cabin was starting to cool down. Good thing he had planned for this cold snap. He left the kitchen and lumbered up the hall that separated the bedrooms on either side. The cabin was not wide, but it was long. Lots of room to spread out. He allowed his hood to fall off while making his way into the living room. He was pulling his heavy, feather-filled jacket from his arms, about to throw it over the back of the overstuffed couch when he sensed something was out of place. *It's just me,* he mused, *I'm really worn.*

He would sit down right after he added some more wood to the fire. The embers were still flickering spikes of bright orange ebbs and that familiar crackling tickled his ears. Along with his own voice, those were the only sounds he had to contend with. He rolled his shoulders and shook his hair, which had grown down around his ears. Haircuts had become a non-necessity, and he kind of liked his inattention to grooming, a foray into uncharted land for him. Rubbing his sore neck, he turned ready to rest his weary...

"Anita!"

"Cameron!" Anita staggered to her feet shaking her head vigorously as if trying to rouse herself.

"What..." He looked at her from head to toe. "How did...how did you get here? The storm."

"I was here before it started. Before it started good, anyway." She held on to the back of the couch, using her free hand to rub her stomach.

"Anita. It's not safe for you here." He rushed her, placing his hands firmly on her shoulders. "Where is Har—"

"He's not here."

"I can see that." He released her and began pacing the length of the room. "Where is he, Anita. Did Harold... I mean, does he know you are here?"

"No, Cameron, I came on my own." She leaned down to her elbow. "May I sit again?"

"Anita, I have no idea what you're up to, but you've got to leave. Anything can happen here and in your condition."

"Cameron, I brought myself here." She lowered herself gingerly back on to his generous couch. "And you know I can't leave. Who would come for me in this weather? Your little Jaguar would never make the trip. Not even to town."

Confused and defeated, Cameron realized his curious neighbor would have no reason to come back anytime soon. And he would surely be taking all three of their lives in his hands if he tried to drive his car. If he walked for help it would take forever, and he couldn't leave Anita and her baby. She was right. He was stuck with her, at least for the time being.

"Okay, Anita, you've got me." He plopped down on the chair across from her. "What do you want? And how in the world did you find me?" *And how are you still pregnant?*

There she sat like royalty on his great plaid couch, her belly full of baby, not his. *How dare you invade my sanctuary,* he was about to tell her when he heard, "Don't. Just listen." The message came to him loud and clear: not in words, but a gentle prodding. It was this same urging that caused him to purchase more wood, stock the shed with extra supplies and blankets and that made him go into town this morning for enough food to last a month. *Could He have known about her coming?*

"Well, if you're not going to listen to me, I don't know why you bothered to ask me the question," Anita shrugged.

Cameron roused himself. "What?" he got up pacing.

"You asked me how I located you, and I was saying, 'I found your diary.'"

"My diary. You read my diary," he groused moving away from the fire and toward her. "Do you mean the one that said 'don't read this book' right on the first page?"

Anita nodded gripping the couch armrest, as Cameron pressed closer.

"Contained in that book, Miss Anita, are my hopes and dreams, my fears and ruminations, my apprehensions, my conversations with no one, my conversations with the world. I speak to God, to myself, to the universe." He was leaning nose to nose with her. "You will be perplexed by what you read, astonished, amused and disappointed. Contained there are ramblings, day-joys and night terrors. They are moments, snapshots of what passes through and sometimes sticks. Don't get stuck there, for to know me you must speak to me, hear my cry. You must watch what I do and say. If you are not the Former, the Clay-Maker, the King, you will find here a glimpse and a stone, one will illuminate and the other crush. A puzzle you will attempt to dismantle. You can not, for his maker is the Lord."

His breath seared her face. She had pulled her legs onto the couch and balled into herself. Shrunken, her voice quavered, "What? No, Cameron, I didn't read that. You wrote that... it's beautiful," she whispered. "I'm sorry... I didn't read it." She squeezed her eyes shut and turned her head. "Please, Cameron, you're scaring me."

Cameron backed off, feeling his chest heave and his pulse quicken. He glared at her, small and fragile, then turned and stalked away.

"No...I mean I did read a little, just enough to know where you were. Just the last page. I read only the last page," she pleaded. "I came home and found you not there. To occupy myself I started to clean. I waited weeks then I came desperate."

"Became."

"What?"

"*Became*, you became desperate," he pounded his palm on the fireplace mantle.

"Oh, Cameron, let's not quibble. You know I don't speak the best English when I'm upset."

"Or very comfortable," Cameron said, thinking of her whispered pleas during their lovemaking.

"I wanted to know where you were, and I... I just found it, that's all."

Yes, this was Anita: a quandary, a conundrum, a pure puzzle. He used to like it. He walked over to the front door and pulled it open. Sleet slashed his face.

"I came here for..."

"For what, Anita?" he questioned, not bothering to turn from his view of the tangled mob of snowcapped-trees, a driveway no longer distinguishable from its surroundings and icicles hanging like prison bars. "What could make you come out here in this storm? How do you propose to get back and in your condition? Your baby, Anita, what could you have been thinking?"

"I was thinking—"

"What!" Cameron spun forcefully, toppling Anita who was up and literally on his heels when he whipped around. "I'm sorry." His hands flew, gripping hers, pulling her into himself, and steadying them both by leaning against the wall. His hands betrayed him, massaging her shoulders and wandering down her arms. She felt puffy, supple, lavish. Her belly was hard, but it swerved next to his. Her cheeks were chipmunk-full and her hands, so small. She looked like, like a... skinny teddy bear. He quashed the urge to smile. *She's so cute,* he thought. He was melting. "Sit down, Anita. You must be cold and tired."

"I am, Cameron, but I need..."

"Yes, what do you need?" he asked pulling her coat off her still slender shoulders, sitting her down, and pulling her overly fashionable and weather-worthless boots from her swelling feet.

"Some warm food," she conceded, "please get me something."

"Sure," he said, getting to his feet and pushing back just far enough to take in the full picture of her sinking into the enormous cushions of the davenport he had purchased from the Clays, neighbors some several miles away. She was helpless, and it was in his power to give her solace or to make her life unbearable. He wondered which he would do.

When he returned with chili and chocolate, both hot, she was fast asleep. Cameron went to the bedroom closet and pulled out several blankets and quilts. He covered her securely, tucking in the edges and putting his puffiest pillow under her head. He then sat back in his stuffed armchair and pondered the woman before him. She had been his wife, told him she was pregnant, told him that the baby she was carrying was not his but Harold's, her former lover. What was she doing here? Did she tell anyone she was coming? Who would let her do this? Wasn't Harold's baby overdue? Didn't she know how dangerous this was? Wouldn't she want to be with Harold at a time like this?

There would be no answers tonight. He would try tomorrow.

Walking into the vast darkness of his cold bedroom, he fell face-first into his hard mattress. He was as tired as he had ever been. Not the kind of tired he'd been lately from working until sweat poured from his brow and chilled on his cold face. Nor was this the kind of tired he used to feel from fighting the voice that plagued his soul when he had cursed

God in his mind. This was a new kind of tired: much worse than one and not nearly as bad as the other. It was a wearying, worrying kind of tired, and he wondered how long he'd have to fight one kind of tired or another. Was there no rest for the wicked, even if he wasn't so wicked anymore? Sleep found him shivering in his cotton shirt and jeans, tight boots still gripping his feet.

She was there off in the distance, whispering and whimpering. Her eyes were wide and bright and they blinked at him. Here, I'm here, they called, and he ran to her. "Evelyn, Evelyn, I'm here." Her little hand reached for him and his reached for her. He tried to hold on, but she was slipping away. The pain welled up in him so hard that he cried out, "Evelyn, I'll save you!"

In the other room, Anita twisted into thick blankets and quilts trying to cover her ears. "Cameron, can you go knock on the Thomas' door?" Anita twisted in the covers, her hands searching for him. "Tell them to be quiet," she mumbled. She woke up on a big comfortable couch not the stiff board she was used to in Chicago. Pushing up to her elbows she listened carefully to the sounds coming from the other room. Ah yes, it was Cameron, and she was in Anderson, Wisconsin, not Chicago. She had come to reclaim her husband. But he was in a separate room, crying out for another woman. She sunk back down into the soft couch. She had traveled many hours and many miles to be with him. She had risked her life and the life of her child to reach him, and he called out for Evelyn, probably the woman who kept this cabin so neat. Anita knew it should have been her who kept his life in order, and it was all her fault that it wasn't. She buried her face in the gigantic pillows Cameron had delicately placed beneath her head and cried herself back to sleep. Tomorrow she'd walk to the nearest house or cabin and beg to use their phone to get a ride into town. If she froze to death at least she'd do it with dignity.

CHAPTER 19

New

A cornucopia of food lay before him as the frost from the fridge escaped to greet his sleep-deprived eyes. He'd loved cooking for himself whenever the mood hit him. But with Anita here, he needed to get started right away making their food. He threw half a slab of fresh bacon in a cold cast iron skillet and cranked up the blaze on the wood stove eye. After pouring off the pool of oil that oozed from the meat, he let it sizzle till it was stiff. He removed the bacon and cracked several country eggs into the grease-coated pan. A cloud of dark smoke scented with the sweet aroma of bacon filled the room. He loved it.

He could hear Anita making small groans. She was waking up. He looked around the room reproaching himself. Why, oh why hadn't he gotten a phone while he had the chance, or a more suitable vehicle? The weather was worse than they'd predicted. And even a healthy man could have an emergency. Case in point, Anita asleep on his sofa. She was so overdue. He grabbed the spatula and tossed the slippery black edged eggs onto a serving dish. *Any minute.* He slammed his fist on the wooden counter. *Harold's baby should already be here.*

"Cameron, it's time," he thought he heard from down the hall.

"Coming, Anita, you must be starved. I can put some bread on the griddle for toast," he said, covering the burner. "Only take another minute."

"I'm not hungry, Cameron. I'm telling you it's time—"

"Time for what? Anita, as soon as the weather clears up we've really got to get you to where you can get some help," he shouted.

"We can't. You've got to listen to me," she squealed.

"Listen, for what?" He rummaged through his kitchen drawer pricking the skin under his fingernail on the fork he was reaching for. "Ouch!" he pulled his hand away from the open drawer, shaking it wildly in the air. "You want me to thank you for gracing me with your presence or for, for... what is this you're doing precisely?" He turned the faucet on and rinsed his hands while leaning toward the hall that led to the living room door to hear her better. She'd stopped talking. "Do you want to get back together? Harold walk out on you? Maybe sleeping with him, just after we were married, wasn't such a good idea. Want me to raise his child?"

"Cameron, the baby, it's, it's coming," she rasped.

More games, he thought. "Anita, this is not necessary." He dried his hands on the dishtowel and sauntered toward the living room still wearing his jeans and T-shirt from the night before. "You're here, you have my complete attention."

Where is she? He scanned the room. She stood stooping over the back of a chair, panting heavily. "My... god," he stammered rushing toward her. "Anita, we have to get you out of here!" He panicked, looking this way and that.

"Cameron, we can't. You have to...phew...phew... do it!"

"But Anita, how can I?"

"The books," she blew. "Cameron, you know how," she cried. "You read all those books when I first told you. You know what to do. You told me you did. NOW DO IT!" she yelled, falling to a squat. "It's here, Cameron. Help me."

A flood gushed from her body, while everything in Cameron's body seized. "I...I'll be back, Anita."

"Cameron, where are you going?" she reached toward him. "Please don't. Cameron, pleeeaaase..."

There was blood everywhere, down the sheets where her wrists lay splayed open. He could not stop it. The red oozing, gushing. She lay still, frozen, white, pale. He had only dozed for a minute. Where had she found the knife? He had carefully hidden the only one he had not thrown away. And now she was gone, he was sure of it. Why couldn't he do anything right?

"Anita, you don't understand," he panted, literally seeing red and back to the wall in the adjourning room. "I have to go get help."

"No, you can't leave!"

He jumped up, rummaging frantically over his bedroom chest looking for his car keys. "You don't understand. If I stay, you'll die."

"Mom. Mom." The words echoed deep inside his chest, but no sound crossed his lips. Tears buried inside his soul wrung him dry, but no water wet his face. Pain crumpled the pit of his being, yet he sat bolt straight, eyes strained open. "Useless. I asked you to watch her, to take care of her while I worked. You couldn't even keep her from the knife drawer."

"Cameron, please. Cameron, you... If you leave... Leave, we'll die. We will die!" Her words were jumbled and crazed.

Cameron stumbled to the doorway, staring down the hall toward the kitchen. He braced himself between the walls. He would get the car started, drive to town...

"But Dad, you were gone so long."

"Shut up! Your mother is dead and it's all your fault, you useless, useless boy. God curse you, everything you touch turns to dirt."

IT was hurling toward him: **helpless, useless... I hate you, God... I hate you, Cameron...** His head was splitting, and his breath was catching fast and shallow. Darkness: thick, heavy, oppressive. He reached forward, feeling he could pick it out of the shadows, feeling he could simply embrace it, welcome it back.

"You are delivered in Jesus' name." Mama Rose's words punched a small hole. "When '**IT**' comes back to challenge you, maintain the ground." With his hands planted firmly against the walls, he slid to the floor.

"When an evil spirit goes out of a man, it goes through dry and arid places, looking for a home. Finding none, it returns to its former residence trying to get back in. You have the power to keep it out."

Just as he buckled, the shout, "CAMERON, FIGHT!"

"Satan, you are a liar," he mumbled from his bowed position. "And the truth is not in you." He felt something shift. "I am healed in Jesus' name." His breathing slowed. His back straightened. "I rebuke you in the name of the Lord." He was on his feet.

"Cameron, Cameron, please come back to me. I need you... child needs you. Help us!" He spun toward Anita's voice. "Cameron, please help us. We need you! We can't make it without you..." her voice trailed off. He ran toward it.

His living room looked crystal clear. He spotted Anita on her knees clutching her belly with one hand and holding the floor with the other. "Cameron," she looked up, her face wrung with pain and fear. "We're dying!"

In one huge step he was before her. On his knees, eye-to-eye, nose-to-nose, mouth-to-mouth. "Breathe, Anita." With their lips forming perfect "O's", they breathed as one.

He folded her into his arms and carried her to his mattress. It was hard. *At least Anita and Harold's baby won't be born in a manger,* he thought, which could have happened in this wilderness.

"Cameron, I'm scared. Can you birth *our* baby?"

Our baby. "Don't say that, Anita, you're delirious."

"Save our baby, Cameron, please," she rasped in rapid belts.

"You're hysterical." Why would she taunt him? Surely she knew he would not abandon her and Harold's child out here. She didn't need more lies.

"I hate you! Get this thing out of me!" Now this was the straightforward Anita he knew.

"Wait here." He pried her fingers from his thin shirt and moved quickly into the kitchen. *Childbirth without Fear* raced through his brain. Grantly Dick-Read made it sound simple. Hilarious, nobody could be expected to birth his own child, or, in his case, the baby of his wife's lover. Spit slid down his throat. His brow furrowed as he put on large pots of water to boil. Unwanted pictures of Anita and Harold's entangled legs and bodies assailed him. He dispelled them by pulling antiseptics and cotton cloths from the drawers and humming a lullaby. Fortunately new images and knowledge from the childbirth books emerged, but being "without fear" was as far away from his reality as he could imagine. He was terrified. His hands, pale and shaky began to cut sheets and rip them into strips. He needed something more powerful than Dr. Dick-Read. He needed the Word. He needed God. "Help me," he trembled.

You can do anything with my help. You can deliver this baby. The enormity of the new words settled in slowly. And ever so slowly he felt his strength. "Help me to accept this child as my own if you have sent Anita back to be my wife," he mouthed, pulling all his supplies into a heap and marveling that this prayer was anywhere in him. Even now his stomach reeled and revolted at the thought of giving her a second, no third, or was this a fourth chance? What kind of man could accept another man's child, born just shy of the time his own baby could have been born of the same woman? Was he weak to think of it? Or was this what God intended?

He hurried back to Anita, squeezing in next to her.

"It hurts." She lurched forward gripping the neck of his shirt and a fair amount of his skin.

Despite his own pain he leaned forward, nose-to-nose again. It appeared to comfort her. "I have you, baby, don't worry. I won't let your …er…our child die or you either." At that she fell back onto his thick pillows and blew a huge sigh. Cameron quickly left the room to check his water and sterilize his supplies. He ran back to sneak a peek into the bedroom. Amazingly, Anita appeared to be sleeping. He came in placing tarps strategically about the room. There would be blood and other matter, and this time he'd be ready. Now he sat in the chair at the foot of the bed facing her, waiting. *God help me, God help me*, rolled over and over in his head, and he knew with assurance that God would.

Hair flew. His. She pulled it out in handfuls. And screams. Curdling screams like live animals being skinned emanated from a creature unlike any he had ever known. She had perched her legs on his shoulders, pushing and prodding, begging and pleading for the life to come up and out. He had squeezed her, massaged her, and cajoled her, the woman. He begged, cooed, and coaxed the child. Finally, he realized there was nothing he wouldn't do to save this woman and to get this child born safely. Yet when the baby slid out, it was still… not breathing.

Not again!

CHAPTER 20

Life and Death

The baby was not crying, and Anita was yelling for it. He had done everything just the way they said in the books. She lie propped on his thickest pillows, her knees wide. Clutching the covers, she pushed long and hard every time he commanded and rested when he told her to stop. When the slick black hair of the baby's head shown through, he told her, and they both giggled nervously. "It's almost here, Anita. Our baby's about to be born. Thank you, Lord!" he exclaimed. His heart swelled, than sank when he tied off and cut the cord that joined Anita to the child he had gently turned and tugged from her body. The baby was not moving. As he stared in disbelief, the placenta presented itself and was out. He wrapped and moved it with his free hand. And now the lifeless child lie swaddled and cradled against his bed-sheet-covered chest. He looked at Anita, her arms grasping, her fingers groping, and he yelled, "No, I won't!" He wouldn't. He couldn't bear to give the dead baby to her. As a wife, she had failed him over and over again. Consciously and ruthlessly, she had attempted to stamp the life essence out of him, all because he had dared to love her. But this failure was not hers. It was his. All his study, all his determination had not been enough to save the life he had decimated with his feeble attempt at doctoring. Cameron howled at the realization.

"Please, Cameron." She was shivering. "Please bring him to me." Cameron looked to the baby and started to mumble, then to moan. Suddenly words, unintelligible, rumpled and run-together tumbled forth. Words, so many words, came rushing out. Were these the unknown tongues he had prayed for? He was pretty sure they belonged to no earthly language.

"Sing, Cameron. The baby needs a lullaby. I like your song. Sing to our baby."

He looked over at her, helpless for the first time since he'd known her. Her little hands gripped the covers. They were tight and blood drained. Her knees were up, parted and trembling. Her eyes narrowed, refusing to open. The smell of acrid afterbirth lingered in the air making it hard to think.

He figured she was hysterical, but he had tried everything so he started singing, "Rock-a-by-baby," only the English was unstable, it wouldn't stick. Then the other language began again. This time it flowed freely and he sang, He sang like he had never sang before, he sang like his life depended on it. No... he sang like the life of his... like the life of her baby depended on it.

When his voice started to crack and Anita started to whimper rather than whine, he looked at the baby's closed eyes and surrendered. I can't make this happen. He walked over to Anita and laid the limp child on her chest. She lowered her reddened and puffy eyes to see the babe still and quiet. Cameron knelt next to her, his own eyes bleary and glazed over. "Sing again," she begged.

"I can't," he rasped.

"You must. Your voice will heal him." Cameron wanted to laugh the absurd laugh of the dead. Everything he touched turned to dirt. Isn't that what his father said and wasn't it true? The job at Brandon & Dobbs, the relationship with Shelly, keeping his mother safe, his marriage, and now the delivery of Anita's child. She snagged his hand and laid it on the baby's chest. She placed hers on top. "Sing, Cameron, the baby needs us." So he sang. She sang too. Nothing they voiced was intelligible, but they continued until... until they were joined by a softer tone.

"Anita," Cameron squealed, "the baby's eyes."

"Huh?"

"They're fluttering."

"What color—"

"What?" Cameron looked at the baby, who was not a he at all— but a she.

"What color are his eyes?"

"It's a girl, Anita," he corrected, as her words pierced his thoughts. He peered intently at the baby's flickering eyes. "Green," he muttered, "they are green." Cameron lifted the tiny infant in the air, watching her little legs stretch and feeling her damp skin beneath his touch. His lips quivered as he tried to form words worthy of thanking God, words worthy of thanking His Father for this magnificent blessing, when like a magnificent mallet it came crashing: brown and brown make brown. This baby's eyes were green. "Anita, she's mine. This baby, she's mine."

"Yes," Anita whimpered, "she is yours and mine."

"But how? I thought you said—"

"Cameron, this is our child. I was never with Harold, only you." He landed back on the bed with a thud. He wasn't crazy, he wasn't a failure, and he wasn't an infidel. God loved him. The proof was wiggling in his arms. The blood had not stopped him. His mother was alive in his daughter's eyes.

Anita had been with him nine days since the baby's birth and he had taken adequate care of them both.

He had a family if only for a short time. He was loath to let it go, but the weather was breaking. A doctor really should check Anita and the baby.

His day had been grueling. He had spent sun up to sun down clearing the remaining drift snow and other debris from his meandering gravel drive, about three city blocks from his house to the lead-in road. Miraculously much of the big drifts had melted or shifted away from their small road. He also gave thought to the land, all seventy-five acres, too much for one person, or one family. He wasn't sure what he was going to put on it, but it would be some kind of charitable endeavor. He trusted God would make him aware of what and when. In the meantime he just wanted to be ready. And it felt good to be out of the cabin giving his arms a chance to move and his legs room to stretch. He had never known he could be happy engaging in physical labor. There was so much new to him here.

With darkness settling in, he longed to see his child and her. Walking quickly he soon stood on the thawing porch taking in the scenery and inhaling the crisp air. Here there was no manipulating or maneuvering. You work with the dirt, the sky, and the trees, and if conditions are favorable they yield gain. He was finished with the life that the advertising business promoted. He was no longer the cold and calculating Mr. O'Neil, at least he no longer wanted to be. Cameron O'Neil, father, and perhaps husband, sounded good. Maybe he'd farm and donate most of the food to an organization to feed the poor, or maybe he'd have some of the boys from Kimberlane Steel's budding organization come out and learn how to work the land after he figured it out himself. He grinned, imagining himself with a big straw hat and brown overalls, his pitchfork firmly planted in hand.

Farmer or not, his shoulders ached from clearing the fallen brush which the wind had coaxed from their high boughs. And had he known that shoveling could be a full time job, perhaps he would have gone into a different business from the beginning. He rolled his shoulders, the throbbing indicating he had a long way to go as an outdoorsman. Fatigued and drooping, he was back at his house. He opened the door and found Anita up and straightening. Hummm.

"Hello," he greeted, not really knowing how to address her anymore.

"Good evening, Cameron. You had much work to do today."

It was more a statement than a question. It didn't really require a response. He pulled off his gloves and hat tossing them on the wooden mantle above the fireplace. He put his coat on the metal hook behind the door. "I was clearing the driveway it's time—"

"You want us to go then..."

He could feel his brow knit. What was she talking about now? He had told her his baby was never going to leave him. This was the first she had said regarding Chicago. Why was it that her words, even when calm, were like shards of glass severing his nerves? "I was clearing it because—"

She became wide-eyed and sidestepped him, moving toward the front door. "Cameron, who's that?" she pointed.

He turned to see who Anita was talking about as she squinted toward the window. "Maybe Newberry." He glared past her. "Can't wait to see who he got to look after the place. Seems the man's woefully inadequate. We could be dead by now."

"Maybe he knew you were here, you know, alone. Thought you didn't need anyone to check."

"Maybe, but I've got a feeling these people don't have much else to talk about except what goes on between them." He turned his attention to his child. "How's she sleeping?"

"Come and see." Anita rushed to grab his arm and escort him to their baby. Every time he talked or thought about their daughter, he got a lump in his throat, and he'd never get used to Anita being so accommodating.

They stood in silence hovering over the baby girl's dresser-drawer crib—not exactly a manger, but not far from it. Rude pounding interrupted their silent reverie.

"Mr. O'Neil," the jolly Newberry announced as he bounded through the door. "We've tried everything to get in here. You have one of the most secluded places around. Canny only got around to tellin' me yesterday that there was a pregnant woman here. She okay?"

"Yes, and that's no thanks to any of you," Cameron said flatly.

"There's no need to worry about us," Anita piped in. "My husband delivered our child all by himself. She is beautiful."

"I'll be the judge of that."

Anita and Cameron looked at each other for support and patience, then for the biggest belly laugh that either had enjoyed in a very long time. They guffawed with such vigor they had to lean on each other to remain standing. After laughing until it hurt, they led the tactless man in to see their lovely daughter.

"Wow, she is a beauty. What's her name?"

Cameron and Anita looked to each other.

"She's got a name, don't she..? You city people beat all." He looked from one to the other. "What you been callin' her, 'baby'?" He slapped his thigh and squealed with laughter. "Well, I guess you want to see the doc so he can give baby 'no-name' here a clean bill of health?"

Again nothing. "I can see you need more than you can give. Now I can get Mabel to come out here. She's my wife and the neighborhood midwife. She can look after you or I can get you to the doctor." He paused, "Doctors are expensive... Well, what'll it be?"

"The doctor!" they yelped in unison.

"Just like most city folk." He shrugged. "Well, it's about time I earned my maintenance money," the tardy Newberry announced. "You've gotten along fine this long. I'll have my Mabel come around to-morrow early. She'll pronounce the misses there fit to travel, and I'll take you all to town in the big truck. No charge, agreed?" He extended his ruddy hand.

Cameron would have fired their would-be helper on the spot, except he really wanted to get his family in to see the "city" doctor. "Deal," Cameron agreed, grabbing the silly man's hand.

CHAPTER 21

Our Town

Town seemed so civilized. The streets were plowed, and people were milling about. Many were frequenting the little shops and quaint businesses. It was as if Cameron was seeing the place for the first time. It reminded him of a snow village in a glass ball. He liked it.

The doctor's office was above a five and dime store. It had two examining rooms, a bathroom, and an office. Cameron snatched open closets and cabinets while the doctor and nurse were not looking. He and Anita peeked in to find medicines, tools, attire, bandages, and other standard stuff. They nodded to each other. Their baby could be examined, and, if necessary, treated here. After about twenty minutes of poking and prodding Anita piped up. "Cameron," she spouted with averted eyes and a strange blush, "I need to leave for a while. Will you and the baby be alright while I'm gone?"

"Mrs. O'Neil," the doctor, a kindly old man, balding and round, paused with his spindly fingers still wrapped around the stethoscope. "I won't be much longer here. Surely you can wait a few more minutes."

"I beg to be pardoned, doctor, I cannot wait."

The doctor shrugged and looked to Cameron for help. Only Cameron was long past help. If Anita wished to make some kind of hasty escape, he would only be forestalling the inevitable to try and stop her. He realized now that his power to control anything was certainly long gone. If she was leaving the baby, he could live with that. When she said she had to go, he wondered why she didn't move. She didn't need his permission.

"Cameron." She leaned to tug on her husband's ear. "May I?"

"Yes, Anita, do what you want, I can't stop you."

She bowed her head completely now and left quickly.

"Are they all like that?" The doctor smiled, a little too big for Cameron's taste. He didn't want to irritate the doctor, especially while he was handling his newborn, but he thought this man had better be referring to women in general.

True to his word, in fifteen minutes Dr. Kilabrew gave baby O'Neil a clean bill of health, so Cameron sat on the bench outside his office rocking his cherry-cheeked baby and thumbing through the basket that Kilabrew asked his nurse to retrieve as soon as he saw their baby's torn sheet diapers tied at her sides. In this basket were cloth diapers, large safety pins, three sack suits with sleeves and a draw string at the feet, some soft, white clothes, and a real set of plastic pants. They had been using one of Anita's shower caps with two holes cut for the baby's legs. Cameron smiled thinking, these people think we're indigent, migrant, or just don't care. He'd have to do something about that. "Where is she?" he blurted aloud. And just when his chewing gum was completely out of flavor, she showed up loaded down with packages. He tried not to show his irritation. She went in for her short examination, and soon they were loaded back into Newberry's truck and bouncing back to the cabin.

"Anita," he started when the great pines and the narrow road that led to the cabin emerged, "what was so im..." He trailed off, turning his attention to the heavy snow-white dipping branches, some barely escaping the ground. There would be plenty of time to grill Anita if that's how he chose to spend whatever time he had remaining with her.

"Cameron, when we get home..." Home, how he had wished this could be their home. That was before she ruined everything with her lying and cheating.

Today was just another example of her selfishness, running off to buy herself things, missing the first doctor visit with her baby. Did this woman's conceit know no limits? He really wished she would be more careful with her choice of words.

"Yes, Anita, what is it?"

"I was wondering..."

"What?" He heard the impatience in his own voice. She looked wounded, *but why?*

"Could you, could you..."

"Yes," he softened.

"Could you let me and the baby have a little time in the cabin alone?"

"Sure," he snapped. He would never, as long as he lived, be able to understand her. And he no longer wanted to. He just didn't have the energy. He'd find something to do while she spent her time alone with the baby.

When they arrived at the cabin, Cameron opened the truck door for Anita and took the baby in her plaid shirt blanket from Anita's arms. She was asleep. She was perfect, her olive complexion, her long dark lashes and button-red cheeks, irresistible. He inhaled and swore he could smell her sweetness. He walked her through the toasty living room and into the small bedroom, gently placing her into the makeshift cradle that he and Anita had fashioned out of his large walnut dresser drawer. Her calm breathing soothed his soul. He left without sparing a glance for the child's mother.

Cameron hadn't taken the time to remove his wool coat or shake the ice off his boots. He grabbed a hat and scarf from the cloak tree on his way out, nearly toppling the thing. He stalked from the house without looking back. He was done with crying, done with hoping. He was a changed man, and someday... someday if he could maintain, God would bless him with a woman to love. For fifteen minutes he sloshed around making giant water-puddle footprints when panic sat in. What if Anita took the baby? What if she was plotting a secret escape? What if— No, he was letting his imagination run away with him. She couldn't drive his little car through this mess. Could she drive at all? He didn't know. There were so many things he didn't know about her. So many things he'd never get the chance to know.

Finally, he smothered his reservations and walked the snow white winter-land talking to his father, his real father—from the deepest part of himself—about what he wanted, what he really desired.

When Cameron's feet felt like lead balls and his face felt like stretched leather, he thought it was time to return home. Before the cabin came into view, the sweet smell of something foreign and un-known beckoned him. And though ice had begun to form on his eyes, he could see light flickering in the window. The smell made him want to run to the door, and the light seemed like...like an invitation. He trudged quickly to the door and pushed it open. Taking a small patch of his scarf that wasn't caked with cracking snow, he wiped his eyes. He was sur-prised to see a red and white gingham tablecloth on the sturdy log coffee table and there were blue print plates set on top. He smiled despite himself. What was she up to?

He removed his heavy stuffed coat and scratchy wool flapped-ear hat. He was leaning against the wall about to remove his boots, when he heard, "Don't."

"What now, Anita?" he sighed turning to face her square on.

"I don't want you to. Just walk on the red car-pet." She was barelegged and wearing a pretty cotton dress.

"The red carpet?" He gave his attention to a red blanket flung from the door to the couch. "Okay, I'll play." Maybe she was postpartum-crazy and maybe he'd like that better than 'lady sinister'. With his boots untied but still on, he marched dutifully over to the stuffed couch and sunk in. Anita disappeared back into the kitchen. He was too tired now to care. When he opened his eyes, she was standing before him gripping what appeared to be a large pot of boiling water. *God have I earned this?!* "Anita, what?"

"For your feet," she retorted, kneeling slowly next to him. Carefully, she unlaced his boots and with great effort pulled them from his feet. Then she carefully rolled down his thick white socks, her soft hands stroking his calves as she did. If she was going to kill him, he was weary enough to let her. But he had to ask, "Anita, what is this about?"

"Cameron, I have never made love to you," she said, cutting away his pant legs with scissors she pulled from her dress pocket.

"Anita, we have a child," he managed before dropping his head back on the pillow and swallowing hard.

"Cameron, I have not been a good wife to you."

What! The heck you say. He felt a soft, wet, and cool cloth slip across his feet. The pot had not been boiling after all.

"Hummm," the guttural moan slipped from his throat. He didn't want to like what she was doing. "Anita," he found his voice again, "what are you doing?"

"I am loving you. Now tell me about your dreams. What do you want to make of this place?" She laid her head on his thigh as she carefully rubbed and stroked his aching toes.

"Please don't do this, Anita," he whispered.

"Tell me, my husband, I want to hear it. Tell me how our life will be. Tell me how you and I and our daughter will live here in these woods."

He had heard this before. His neck snapped up and he grabbed her by her shoulders, jerking her up to the couch. "Are you still mocking me, Anita?"

"Cameroon," she moaned, gripping his whiskered face with both her hands.

"Stop it!" he yelled. "Don't call me that. Don't ever call me that."

"But I want to be your wife. Your real wife," she insisted, peering deeply into his eyes. "I want to love you the way you love me. I want to show you that I know how to do things right. I want you to love me again. And I want to be lost in your love. So I beg you, my husband, tell me everything. Tell me about your pain and your sorrows. Tell me about what makes you happy."

"Anita, I feel like I've waited a lifetime to hear you say these things, but they are just words, words from the most unrelenting, hurtful person I've ever known. Please just leave me alone."

"I've done it, haven't I? I've lost you."

"Yes, I think you have." Cameron eased up from the couch, walked barefoot to the fireplace, picked up a poker and stared, paralyzed, into the flames.

CHAPTER 22

What's The Word

Anita was undone. She had come here to save her marriage, to save her life. But she failed, everywhere failure, everything failure. She ran from the living room, where Cameron stood staring at the fire and into the bedroom. She walked over to the bed and collapsed near the drawer-cradle where she and Cameron's baby slept. "I'm so sorry, little one," she wept. "Your mother is a failure. I've turned your father away and destroyed your chance to have what I took for granted. I'm so, so sorry."

Her baby girl lay there so softly snuggled in little blankets that she and Cameron had crafted out of his flannel shirts and worn quilts. She hadn't known he owned such things. So much she didn't know. She had wasted so much time being the enemy of the man that she wanted so desperately to love her. "Why God!" she howled. She paced the length of this room, two times bigger than the one in their

Chicago home, wringing her hands and rubbing her arms. She'd be leaving soon. "Why?" she looked toward the ceiling petitioning Him, the one she thought she never would. "Why if you are so real and so powerful have you killed me while I live?"

A river rushed down her face. She put her sleeves to her eyes. The thin fabric did not absorb her grief. A flood came from her nose, and she couldn't find handkerchiefs, tissues...anything. There, she rushed to grab a large gold towel, which seemed to appear from nowhere. She yanked it, causing a large black book to tumble from the nightstand and on to the floor. She marched over and snatched it up. A Bible. His Bible. She started to hurl it, but her sticky fingers stuck to the thin tissue pages. Maybe she'd rip some out to wipe her nose. As she contemplated her divine sacrilege, curiosity seized her. *What's in here? What makes him read it?*

Cameron looked down at his legs. She had actually cut his pant legs away—so Anita. And she massaged his feet. She had never done that before. And she wanted to know his plans. She said she wanted to be part of them.

"Cameron."

"Anita." He jumped at the sound of her voice.

"You said you could not, would not believe my words. Will you believe His? I have something to say to you. Will you listen?"

He ran his hands through his long hair. "Please, Anita, just leave me alone."

"Not until you hear me."

She moved close to him and whipped something from behind her back. A book.

"I know who you are now, and I agree..." Then she took the Bible in both of her small hands and began to read, "Because those who are led by the Spirit of God are sons of God. For you did not receive a spirit that makes you a slave again to fear, but you received the Spirit of sonship. And by Him we cry, 'Abba, Father.' The Spirit himself testifies with our spirit that we are God's children."

What was her game now? Did she plan to use the Word against him? He moved to take the Bible from her. She held her hand against his chest. "Let me finish... 'Now if we are children, then we are heirs—heirs of God and co-heirs with Christ, if indeed we share in His sufferings in order that we may also share in his glory.'"

She paused. "I have made you suffer. And I am so sorry."

Tears filled Anita's eyes and gushed out. Cameron's mind reeled. He suddenly realized he had never actually seen her cry. Lots of clouds, never any rain.

"Cameroon, I know who you are." She stepped toward him. "You are a son of God, and you are the man I love."

Tears or no tears, no matter how hard he tried he didn't trust her. He wanted to feel it, to believe her. But she was evil, crafty beyond anything he'd ever imagined, and she had made him suffer. She had nearly destroyed him. He was recovering well, thinking of other things. To let her back in, to be vulnerable again, to let her kick him one more time was unimaginable.

"I'm sorry Anita," he rasped, "I thought maybe I could for our daughter's sake. I just can't." He turned to walk away. He heard her steps on the hard wood floor as she walked back toward the bedroom door. Good, he thought. Silence and then…

"He wants you to forgive."

He whipped around. It didn't sound like Anita.

"God says—"

"Stop it, Anita. Do you realize what you are doing? Don't pretend—"

"Forgive him, Cameron, for taking your mother away too soon."

"What? Stop it. You don't know what you're doing!"

She was crying, and her lips were trembling. "Help me, Lord," she whispered. Then, "He wants you to forgive yourself. You couldn't save her."

Cameron wanted to slap her. What did she know about any of this? He'd never spoken to her about his mother. She never gave him the chance.

"This is a dangerous game you're playing, Anita. Did you read more of my diaries?"

She shook her head pitifully and kept right on talking, "Forgive David. He was wounded and confused."

He clutched her shoulders and thought he might throw her across the room. Instead he looked into her eyes, deep into her eyes. Maybe he could rouse her before they both did something they'd regret. She seemed to come to herself and nearly collapsed into his arms. Looking more like herself, she looked up and into his eyes.

"Please forgive me, Cameron. I want to be your wife. Will you let me try?"

He couldn't speak. He wouldn't.

"God help me," Anita cried looking toward the ceiling. "I want your son to love me again."

"Anita," he snatched her. If she were lying he'd hate her forever. She draped herself around him, burying her face in his chest.

"He says your healing is in forgiveness. You don't have to keep me as your wife, Cameron. I will go away if you want. But please forgive me. He wants you to. And I want you to. I want you to be healed of the pain I've caused you. Let me go now. I'm not worth all this trouble. I promise I'll never hurt you again."

Cameron released her and pushed her gently away. "You will. You will hurt me again."

"You're probably right." She sniffled and turned to walk away. "I'll start getting my stuff together. But Cameron—"

"And I'll probably hurt you too. It's what people do. It's human nature."

"I see. What about our daughter?" She was wobbly, holding on to the doorframe for support.

"I'll never do it on purpose though." He walked over and pulled Anita to his chest. She wrapped her arms around his body.

"I love you, Anita. And I forgive you. If you can forgive me, we will begin again."

"I love you, Cameron, and I…I…I forgive you too."

Cameron awoke with a start and a horrible sense of loss. He felt through the covers lying next to him on the couch looking for his wife. Anita had been in his arms begging him to love her. Where was she? He jumped to his feet stubbing his toe on the coffee table as he did. He grabbed his foot and stifled an urge to howl, then he stumbled desperately to his bedroom, his heart thundering, beating to the point of bursting. He hurled himself through the bedroom door, searching the dark for her.

Where are you? He was about to yell when he spotted her. Steadying himself against the doorframe, the hammering in his chest slowed. Anita was sitting on the foot of the bed, thick blankets wrapped around her shoulders. When his eyes adjusted to the light, he spotted their baby wiggly and restless, trying desperately to locate her mother's breast. He stood staring at them for a long time, feeling a little like an intruder.

"Come here, husband. Right here." She patted the spot next to her. "This is your place."

He walked over and sat, putting his arm around them both, and pulling them into his side.

"I know what you did with the money from the Colless deal."

Cameron stiffened.

"Mark told me," she continued.

Mark didn't know the whole story. Cameron wondered what he told Anita and if she'd trust Mark's story above his own. "What'd he tell you?"

"He said you tried to give the money back," she slurred wearily, "the money you got from the side deal."

"Anita, I was wrong to…"

"Don't." She raised her finger to his lip then let it drop to her lap. "I didn't want to believe you were good. You are good. . ," she managed, before closing her eyes completely, her head beginning to bob. Cameron laid her gently back and took their purring babe from her arm. He thought about the gifts he'd been given: his sanity, his wife, his child, and the church. All he could think to offer the Lord was his life, but he had something more practical to offer the girls.

He put his pink-faced baby girl back into her makeshift bassinet and pulled the soft covers up around her neck. Next he eased Anita up into the bed and covered her. Tiptoeing into the bathroom, he pulled on the chain above the mirror, then turned his head this way then that, rubbing the prickly brown-blond stubble of the on-again, off-again beard he had grown since his stay in the "wilderness." He pushed at the long hair hanging about his neck and over his ears. He had turned into a scruffy green-eyed grizzly. He opened his drawer and flicked through nail- clippers, lotions, and mouthwash, looking for scissors, shaving cream, and a razor.

"Cameron," Anita sniffled, "please come back to me. Please..." She was kicking and writhing in her sleep.

"I'm here," he said getting under the covers and gathering her to himself. "I'm here, Anita. I'll never leave you, and you'll never leave me."

"No, Cameron, I never will." She reached to stroke his cheek, "Not even till the end of time." They cozied into the layers of cover and slept.

Cameron woke first. He stared at Anita, unable to believe how far his life had come over the course of the past several months. Anita and his baby were with him. He walked his finger over her lower lip.

"Cameron." She stirred, reaching her hand up to caress his face. "Cameron." Her eyes fluttered. "What have you done?"

He clutched her hand. "You like it?"

"Don't take this wrong, I do. I liked your fuzzy look, too, but this is the face I fell in love with. Are you angry?"

"You mean am I jealous of me?" He smiled. "No. But Anita, don't take this wrong. This is what I've prayed for, but I don't get it. Tell me, what happened? You say the 'face' you fell in love with as if this has not just happened. I accept it. How can I not? But I don't understand it."

"My love." She propped herself up, reached for and kissed his hand. "I'm such a stupid child. I don't mean to confuse you. I thought love meant getting my way all the time, so when my father withheld Haruto from me, I thought he didn't love me anymore. And then you came. I knew you to be ruthless and cunning. I recognized the same thing in me. I just didn't understand, that also like me, you wanted out. The strange thing is you thought I could help you. Silly man, I could not help myself."

She ran her hand down his chest. "I know the moment that I realized I loved you."

"Tell me."

"It was when I was desperate enough to make up a child to keep you. Then desperate enough to lie to you about that baby when I thought I was losing you."

He looked down as if the memory still stung.

"Cameron." Anita nudged his chin up with her finger. "I was a child, I thought as a child, but now I'm a woman." She smiled big. "Your strange green eyes have captured me. I want what a woman wants."

He grabbed her hand and pressed his body to hers. "Not yet, it's too soon."

"Not that." She hit his chest. "I want real love from a real man...a man like my father," she whispered. "Can you give me that?"

"You know I can."

"Then let's start... Tell me about our life here in our woods."

Cameron smiled until his jaws ached. He sat up in the bed and pulled Anita to his bare chest, wrapping his arms around her. He looked over to the drawer where his baby lay. "Well first, I'm going to teach you to clean."

"I know how."

Cameron eased her back and looked at her with a smirk.

"No really. Haven't you seen it around here?"

This time he raised an eyebrow.

"Okay, wrong question. What have you not seen?"

When he still looked puzzled she said, "My mess. You have not seen my mess and you have not seen yours. I've been making sure there is no mess."

"That's true, I guess." His smile was brilliant.

"And I'm going to use the supplies I bought in town and show you what real clean looks like. I also bought some good cooking utensils. I'll make you some good food. My mother taught me how. And I got some baby things. Our baby has a pacifier and some real clothes."

"But I thought, I thought Dan had finally picked up the supplies that I asked him to get."

"No. I did, when I left you with the doctor. I also called my parents. They were worried sick, but they forgave me when I told them that I had our baby and that I intended to come back to you."

"Back to me," Cameron swallowed hard. "So you didn't get anything for yourself."

"What do I need? I have everything. And you should fire Dan Newberry. Cameron," she sighed, "I'm going to make you a very good wife." She snuggled closer. "Now be serious and tell me about our life together."

"Anita."

"What?"

"I believe you love me."

"I told you I did."

Pure Poetry

"My love is a snowflower born late, up from the ashes, out of due season, in through the mist. I waited for her to come but she never did, no matter how long I waited, it seemed she never would. I waited and waited like a man dying of thirst, I waited for water; still she did not come to quench my thirst. Just when I thought I'd faint waiting, she came; and when she came, she came and came again."

"Cameroon, what a silly man you are." Anita turned on her pillow to touch his lip. "Such shameful poetry coming from your pretty mouth."

Cameron smiled, and continued tracing circles on her stomach with his finger. "I didn't mean it like that. Besides, it's only shameful if it comes from unfaithful lips."

"Speaking of that... who is Evelyn?" Anita twisted in the covers toward him. "You can tell me now."

"Certainly not a girlfriend." He twisted sideways to meet her eyes. "I have not looked at another woman since the day I made up my mind for you. I don't know any women named Evelyn." He lay back again, placing his hand behind his head. Anita was nestled in the crook of his other arm, so close she felt like an additional appendage. He tightened his hold on her.

"Listen, she's starting to whimper."

"Phew, I'm glad. Anita, are they supposed to sleep that long?"

"I don't know. You read all the books." Anita swung her legs over the side of the bed and started to go for her daughter.

"Don't." Cameron planted his hand on her arm. "I've got it."

Moments later he waltzed over to Anita. "Here she is. Baby O'Neil." His pinky was in the baby's mouth, her pouty cheeks satisfied with her father's pacifier.

Cameron's hair was ruffled and his muscles hewn from country living. He was beautiful to Anita, but it wasn't physical. He had explained to her how hard it was for him to love. It was because of all the love that had been stripped from him, first by his mother, who could not care for him, then by his father who would not. Because of the ugly things being said in his mind—though he rejected them and refused to act on them—he didn't even think God could love him. Then there was her...she sighed. That was all behind them now. God did love him, and so did she. Finally truth.

She reached for her snugly-swaddled babe. "Poor baby. Cameron!" Anita yelped, "Our baby has no name. Twelve days, and no name. We must be terrible parents."

Cameron closed his eyes, smiled, and put his hands behind his head as he lay next to his girls.

Her little hand reached for him, and his reached for her. The pain welled up in him so strongly that he cried out, "Evelyn, I'll save you!"

Cameron bolted upright.

"Are you okay, Cameron?" Anita scrambled up, her arm tight around their daughter. "What is the matter?"

"Anita, I dreamed of her before she was born. God was telling me that I could do it; that I could save our daughter. You asked me who Evelyn was... When you first came here I dreamt I was chasing a little girl with bouncing brown hair and green eyes. And now I've caught her." His smile was brilliant. "Evelyn, I remember now, was my mother's middle name. Our daughter is Evelyn O'Neil. No," he paused, "Evelyn Akiko O'Neil. Do you like it? My mother's middle name and your mother's first name."

"Yes, I love it. She is our little promise from your God."

"Our God." He smiled.

"Yes, our God. He has saved me too." Anita reached for her husband's hand and squeezed. "Evelyn Akiko O'Neil. I love it!"

"I have written
you in the palm
of my hand."

Thank you, God, I believe you.

Are you part of a book club?

Here are some discussion-starters you may wish to use. Also, this author loves to do "home visits," and you never know when I'll be in your town!

1. What attracted you to *Love Promises*?
2. Why do you believe this book has its title?
3. Which character did you like the most, and why?
4. Which character did you least appreciate, and why?
5. Have you read, *Love Changes* or *Love Dreams*?
   a. How does Cameron compare to the other male protagonists?
   b. How is Anita similar or different than the other female protagonists?
6. This story is part of *The Love Trilogy*. How has this story or the others influenced your definition of love?